™

Praise for Jackie Braun

'A great storyline, interesting characters and a
fast pace help immerse readers in this tender tale.'
—RT Book Reviews on
Inconveniently Wed!

'Quite humorous at times,
with beautifully written characters, this is a terrific read.'
—RT Book Reviews on
A Dinner, A Date, A Desert Sheikh

'Solidly plotted with an edgy,
slightly abrasive heroine and an equally unforgettable
hero, this story is a great read. Don't miss it.'
—RT Book Reviews on
Confidential: Expecting!

'…reading her books [is] a delightful experience that
carries you from laughter to tears and back again.'
—Pink Heart Society on
Boardroom Baby Surprise

The Road Not Taken

Jackie Braun

MILLS & BOON

First published in Great Britain 2011
by Mills & Boon, an imprint of Harlequin (UK) Limited,
Eton House, 18-24 Paradise Road, Richmond, Surrey TW9 1SR

© Jackie Braun Fridline 2011

ISBN: 978 0 263 88375 6

Harlequin (UK) policy is to use papers that are natural, renewable and recyclable products and made from wood grown in sustainable forests. The logging and manufacturing process conform to the legal environmental regulations of the country of origin.

Printed and bound in Spain
by Blackprint CPI, Barcelona

Also by Jackie Braun

Inconveniently Wed!
A Dinner, A Date, A Desert Sheikh
Confidential: Expecting!
Boardroom Baby Surprise

Did you know these are also available as eBooks?
Visit www.millsandboon.co.uk

TM

For my good friend Richard Noble.
What would a book signing be without you?

PROLOGUE

JAKE MCCABE CURLED HIS HAND into a fist.
Pain and useless rage had him wanting to
use it. On a wall or whatever else might be
handy. Bloody and bruised knuckles would
be a small price to pay if they brought him
even a small measure of relief.

Instead, he relaxed his grip enough to pick
up a pen and open the journal. It had only
one entry, written a couple of months earlier when the department shrink first recommended keeping a diary as an outlet for his
thoughts and emotions.

"This is crap," it read. "I don't see how
writing things down will make a bit of
difference."

Now, however, with a new wound fester-
ing, he penned the words he couldn't bear
to voice. He didn't find peace in doing so,
for that was impossible. But it turned out the

shrink was right about his need for an outlet. The words flowed in a bitter torrent. One paragraph, then two, scratched in his slashing penmanship.

Afterward, Jake lowered his head and wept. Tears smeared the ink, turning the first sentence illegible. It didn't matter. He would remember the words long after the raging storm of his emotions quieted.

"Miranda killed our baby today."

CHAPTER ONE

THE CAR HIT THE SNOWBANK with enough force that the air bag deployed. But at least it had stopped after what seemed like an eternity of swerving and fishtailing on the maple-tree-lined two-lane highway.

Caroline Franklin Wendell peeled her fingers from the steering wheel and ran one shaking hand over her face. It wasn't her life that had flashed before her eyes during those seemingly endless moments of terror. It had been her son's. She'd nearly failed Cabot by dying and leaving it to his father and grandmother to raise him. That thought had her shivering.

Caro gazed out the windshield. The front end of the subcompact was buried to mid-hood in a snowdrift. But she knew her life had gone off track long before she'd hit that patch of ice. It had been skidding out of control ever since she'd foolishly married Truman four years earlier. She'd just refused to believe it. She'd refused to believe that the mistake she'd made couldn't be fixed.

Even that morning, heading back to him in defeat, she'd held out hope that she would find a way out of this nightmare. Not for her sake, but for Cabot's. Her son was the only good thing to come from her marriage to the heir of one of New England's most affluent and powerful families.

Now, with her heart hammering and her limbs still shaking, she laid her forehead against the faux-leather steering wheel and finally accepted the truth. Truman was right. There was no way out.

I'm doing this for your own good. You need me, Caroline.

Caro wasn't sure how long she'd sat there, only that the last of the heat had leaked from the inside of the car. She could see her breath each time she exhaled and, even through her cashmere-lined leather gloves, her fingertips pinched and prickled from the cold. She fished her cell phone from her purse. Eventually, she would have to call her husband to report her delay and, if need be, beg him for more time. She wasn't above begging when it came to her son. First, she needed a wrecker for her car and someplace warm for her to wait for repairs.

She flipped open her phone and stared for a moment at the photo of her son on the display. He was smiling, happy and free of cares, just as every toddler should be. She ran the tip of her index finger over his cherubic face and then frowned as she realized that her phone had no service.

After forcing open the car door and stepping into the knee-deep snow, she raised the cell high in the air and turned in a semi-circle.

Still nothing.

She stuffed the phone into the pocket of her parka and cursed. The mild oath floated away on a puff of white air.

She could wait for help, she supposed. Although it was doubtful another driver would be foolish enough to be out in these conditions. Only desperation had forced her to be. She glanced down the road in the direction she'd come. She'd passed a gas station when she'd unwisely decided to leave the interstate, as road conditions there had worsened. That was three miles back or maybe four. She was wearing boots, but the supple leather and three-inch heels weren't meant for this kind of weather, much less a rigorous hike in it.

She gazed in the opposite direction. What lay ahead on the road she'd been traveling?

Her luck it would be miles of nothing but more maple trees and snowdrifts. She'd survived the accident but, quite literally, she wasn't out of the woods yet. Tears stung her eyes and her breathing grew labored as panic kicked into high gear. What was she going to do? She had a deadline to meet.

Caro thought she heard bells, a rhythmic jangling from off in the distance. She dismissed the sound as the product of the wind and her own imagination. A moment later, though, a man on horseback appeared at the bend in the road. The rim of his hat was covered in snow, as were the broad shoulders stuffed inside a tan shearling coat. He looked like something out of a dream. A fantasy, she amended, as he drew closer and his ruggedly handsome features came into focus: deep-set eyes of an indiscernible color, angular cheekbones and a shadow of a beard on the lower half of his face.

Caroline's heart knocked out an extra beat

at the same time her knees gave way, and she sank into the snow.

Clearly, she had died.

Jake wiped a gloved hand over his eyes after he spotted the woman. She was a vision. Had to be. No one in her right mind would be out in this godforsaken weather. The only reason he was out was to work off the worst of his temper. And he'd had the good sense to tramp about on horseback. The big animal knew her way back to home and shelter even better than he did.

When he saw the woman collapse, he was out of the saddle before his horse came to a stop, trudging the half-dozen steps through a knee-deep drift to reach her. He crouched beside her, resisting the urge to scoop her up in his arms.

Protect and serve.

A lifetime ago, those words had been part of his daily mantra. No longer.

"Lady, hey, lady!" His words sawed gruffly through the wind. "Are you okay?"

She gazed at him with glazed eyes and a look of terror and revulsion. He wasn't insulted. He'd had that effect on people before.

But then she did something that shocked him to his core. She raised one shaky hand to the side of his face and asked, "Are you an angel?"

The question took him by surprise. Jake had been called a lot of things during the past year. Angel wasn't among them.

"Not even close."

"I thought…"

"Are you hurt?"

She blinked, frowned. "I guess not."

"You're sure you didn't hit your head or anything?" He glanced past her into the car and noted the deflated air bag. It had saved her from greater impact, but that didn't mean she hadn't sustained injury.

"I'm okay," she insisted. As if to prove the point, she struggled to her feet.

Jake rose with her. The woman was taller than he'd first thought she would be, given her otherwise delicate appearance. Not delicate, he decided. Fragile. There was a difference.

The top of her head came even with the bridge of his twice-busted nose. He couldn't see her feet through the snow, but he'd bet she was wearing heels, something high and impractical to go along with the rest of her fashionable, if nonfunctional, wardrobe. It was a good thing he'd come along. She wouldn't have lasted another hour out here on her own.

People need you, Jake.

"My car is another matter," she was saying. "I'm not sure the extent of the damage, but it will need to be towed to a garage for a look."

People are counting on you, Jake.

He banished the words as he surveyed the small vehicle. It probably got great gas mileage, but that was about all it had to recommend it. His tone was more gruff than he intended when he said, "You call that a car? It looks more like a toy."

The woman laughed, but the sound verged on hysteria rather than mirth. Make that *half* an hour that she would have survived without his intervention.

"Yes, well, do you know if there is a garage nearby? And a working phone? My cell isn't getting a signal out here. I need to call for a wrecker."

"You can call from the inn."

"Inn?" She sighed and her expression turned hopeful. "There's an inn nearby?"

He nodded. "It's about a half mile up the road."

"Do you know if it has a vacancy?" She grabbed his arm. "Please tell me yes."

Jake swallowed and for just a moment found himself lost in a pair of wide hazel eyes. "I'm sure there's something available."

In truth, the inn was a broken-down husk of its former self, much like the man who'd purchased it a while back. It was closed to the public, but he did have guests this Easter weekend. He was, begrudgingly, entertaining his entire family, a fact that explained why he could be found out in a snowstorm at the moment.

His parents, brother, sister-in-law and their kids had arrived unannounced the day before. Already he and his younger sibling were at odds. He'd left to avoid saying something he was bound to regret. Well, regret more than what had already passed through his lips.

"Thank God," the woman was saying. "I...I don't suppose you could take me there?" Her gaze cut to his horse. Despite the nasty conditions, Bess stood patiently a few feet away. The Clydesdale normally pulled the inn's sleigh and she'd been thrown in with the sale. As angry as Jake had been when he stomped out of the inn, he'd had the presence of mind to take the big animal rather than stalk off on his own.

"Be happy to."

He didn't sound happy, a fact that wasn't lost on her if her expression was any indication.

"You said it's only half a mile. I...I can walk." She took an awkward step forward in the snow.

"Right." He snorted and motioned with one gloved hand. "In those impractical clothes? Hell, lady, you'd be lucky if you didn't freeze to death before you made it ten yards."

She whirled back to face him. Those hazel eyes snapped with heat now, and the color in her cheeks wasn't all the result of the bitter wind. "I'm not helpless! I refuse to be helpless!"

The shouted words echoed off the maple trees, sending some snow down from their branches. Not helpless maybe, Jake thought. But she was desperate. He'd seen that look in the faces of people whose loved ones were caught up in the drug trade. In their cases, he knew exactly what had put it there. But what did a woman who looked like a walking advertisement for the life of the idle rich have to make her desperate?

He dismissed the question, squelched the old urge to offer to help. *Not my problem.* Jake was officially out of the hero business… not that he'd had much choice in the matter.

Even so, he heard himself saying, "Come on. I'll give you a boost into the saddle."

The woman eyed the big animal. This time it was fear rather than pride he heard when she said, "I really don't mind walking."

"Yeah, well, I do. It will take twice as long. At least." This time he tempered his tone. "Don't worry about Bess here. She's a gentle giant."

The woman pointed back toward her car. "What about my bag?"

It was all he could do not to roll his eyes. "How big is it?"

"I don't need the luggage that's in the backseat if that's what has you worried. But I'd appreciate the toiletries bag that's on the floor on the front passenger side."

He glanced through the window and grimaced. It was small enough to fit the definition of a carry-on at the airport, but since this short trip was going to be precarious enough without adding baggage, he said, "I'll have to come back for it."

He expected her to argue, but she didn't. Instead, she trudged through the snow to the horse. Over the howl of the wind, Jake thought he heard her chant, "I can do this. I can do this. I can do this."

He helped her into the saddle before swinging up behind her. Bess shifted, unaccustomed to accommodating one rider on her back, much less two. He knew how she felt. He wasn't accustomed to riding alone, much less with a beautiful stranger all but seated on his lap.

"Steady now, girl. It's all right," he said, reaching around the woman to give the mare's thick neck a reassuring pat. "Just give us a chance to get settled."

The woman turned toward him. "I just realized that I know your horse's name, but not yours."

"It's Jake. Jake McCabe." He braced for her reaction. For a while his name had been synonymous with Satan, at least back in his hometown of Buffalo. But her expression never changed.

"I'm Caroline...Franklin." Her tone

sounded oddly defiant when she added, "My friends call me Caro."

"Well, Caro, are you ready?"

She nodded and they set off.

It took longer than he'd expected to get to the inn and not only because he went a little slower than he would have if he'd been in the saddle alone. The conditions definitely had worsened. The wind had nearly erased the horse's earlier tracks.

He let out a sigh of relief when he spotted the inn, dilapidated as it had become. The place had a soothing effect on him, nestled as it was in a stand of towering trees and out of view of the main road. The wide porch was covered with several inches of snow, even though he'd shoveled it off not long before leaving. In the summer, he envisioned it dotted with the rocking chairs he'd been making in his workshop.

He'd always enjoyed woodworking, and he was pretty good at it thanks to his father's patient tutelage while he was growing up. Where some cops turned to alcohol to unwind after a bad day, Jake had turned to his band saw, sander and other tools of the trade.

He credited them with saving his sanity

last year while he'd awaited the outcome of the internal affairs investigation that had followed the fatal shootings of a woman and her child. They'd been killed during a raid on a house where a major drug dealer was believed to be hiding. Jake hadn't pulled the trigger, but he'd been the one in command.

His team had gone to the wrong address.

Before the investigation was complete he'd crafted two chairs. He'd taken more care with his design and workmanship than ever before, determined not to overlook any detail. He didn't need the department's shrink to tell him it was about regaining control. In the end, he was satisfied with the chairs, but left reeling by the department's findings.

They claimed he'd been given the correct address, but had misread it. No way, was his first reaction. He'd done no such thing. But certain paperwork went missing and, haunted as he was by the tragic deaths, he could no longer be sure. After the inquiry, an official reprimand went into his permanent file, but he was allowed back to work. No other action was to be taken, but then things took an even uglier turn.

The rookie cop who'd fired the shots committed suicide, unable to handle having the blood of two innocent people on his hands. In the court of public opinion, Jake was responsible for that, as well.

In Buffalo, where he'd worked as a police officer for nearly a dozen years after graduating from college with a degree in criminal justice, he'd become a pariah. Oh, some folks rallied around him, both in public and on the force. And the union had vowed to fight the investigation's outcome. But when the captain came to Jake and quietly offered a severance package, he'd accepted it. In truth, he'd already planned to walk away.

He hadn't seen the point in fighting. A woman was dead. Her baby killed along with her. A rookie dead. Even if Jake hadn't screwed up the address, it had happened on his watch. And then there was Miranda...

So he'd packed up and gone, not only from the force but also from Buffalo.

Six months ago, he'd stumbled across the inn. His family had gone there a lot when he was a boy, both in summer and winter. It was located in the shadow of Camel's Hump in Vermont's Green Mountains. He'd loved the place back then and he'd been hoping it would hold the same magic for him as an adult. But it wasn't open for business, and a for-sale sign had been stuck out front. One look at the inn's sorry state and Jake's heart had sunk, but that hadn't stopped him from buying it.

The local people were the same as he remembered them being: polite, if a little standoffish to outsiders. That was fine by him. He wasn't there to make friends. He just wanted peace. He wasn't, as his brother claimed, running away from his problems and hiding out.

"Is this…is this it?"

It took Jake a moment to realize that the horse had bypassed the inn and stopped at the door to the small outbuilding that housed her stall.

"I guess Bess is ready to get out of the storm, too."

"She lives here?" Caro turned in the saddle then so she could see his face. "*You* live here?"

"I do. I own it."

Her brows shot up, and no wonder. Not only was he not the friendly owner one would expect of such a small establishment, he knew the place didn't look habitable with its peeling paint, loose boards and overgrown shrubbery.

"It's not open for business right now. But it's warm and dry. I'll see that you're settled inside before I go back for your bag." He spoke to the horse then. "Sorry, girl, but your day's not through."

It was snowing harder now. The flakes so big it was as if the heavens were engaged in a snowball fight. He hopped out of the saddle and reached for Caro. Even through the bulk of her clothing, he could tell her waist was small and she barely weighed what a child would. She was probably on some silly diet, eating only fruit or drinking special shakes. Women, he thought on a sigh. He'd never figure them out, not that he'd had much practice trying lately.

When they reached the relative safety of the back porch, Caro smiled at him. Surely his dry spell was what accounted for the kick of interest he experienced. Her expression wasn't born of anything more than politeness, yet he found it sexy and a little too inviting.

It didn't hurt that she was saying, "Don't go."

"Don't go?" he repeated absently as he took in her flushed cheeks.

"Nothing in that bag is important. The

weather…" She swept a hand through the air. "You've done enough already. I'd feel horrible if something happened to you on my account."

Jake blinked at her. He'd almost forgotten what it felt like to have someone—a woman—worry about him.

"Are you sure?"

She nodded and bits of melting snow shook loose from her damp hair. He reached out to free some more and she shivered. Her gaze slid to the side, giving him the impression her reaction wasn't completely due to the cold. Interest, as unwelcome as the late-winter storm, stirred a second time. It had been a while since he'd been with a woman, but he recalled perfectly what he was missing.

The door swung open behind them before he could do anything he'd have to apologize for. He was grateful until he realized it was his mother standing there. Her hands were planted on her hips and the look on her face would have left a drill sergeant shaking in his boots.

"Jacob Robert McCabe, don't you ev—" Doreen McCabe halted her diatribe midword as soon as she spied Caroline. Blinking in surprise, she switched gears and tones. "Oh, hello. I'm Doreen. Jake's mother."

"This is Caroline Franklin," he said.

"Caro."

"Right. Caro."

Doreen nodded, splitting her gaze between the pair of them. "I didn't realize Jake was expecting company."

"I wasn't," he said at the same time Caro replied, "I'm not."

"Company, that is." Her laughter was tight.

If his mother found the situation confusing, she didn't let it show. Using the same tone that had kept him toeing the line for the first eighteen years of his life, she shouted, "Good heavens, son! Have you no manners at all? Bring that poor girl inside before she catches her death of cold. She needs to get out of those wet clothes."

Jake swallowed hard, because for one foolish moment, he'd been thinking the same thing.

CHAPTER TWO

CARO STEPPED INTO the vestibule through the door Doreen held open and all but sighed when the warm air greeted her. But what caught her attention were voices. There were several of them, including the high-pitched squeal of children. She sent a quizzical glance in Jake's direction, before bending down to unzip her boots. Numb fingers made her progress slow.

"I thought you said the inn wasn't open for business," she murmured.

"It's not." Jake had already removed his hat. Now, he shucked off his coat.

He didn't sound happy.

"Oh, those aren't guests. They're the rest of our family," Doreen informed Caro as she took her son's coat. With a meaningful glance at Jake, the woman added, "And because we're family, we invite ourselves if need be."

"Mom…"

"Just saying." She took Caro's parka, as well, hanging them both on pegs to dry. "I'll grab some towels for the two of you. Go into the main living area and sit by the fire to warm up while I'm gone."

Caro nearly smiled. Jake didn't seem the sort of man to take orders, but this *was* his mother. Sure enough, he led her to a room at the front of the inn, where a fire blazed in the hearth. An older man was seated in an overstuffed chair next to it. He was reading a book and smoking a pipe. A couple of children, neither of whom was much older than her Cabot, played at the older man's feet. On the couch across from them, a young couple snuggled together under a thick knitted throw.

Family.

An ache welled inside Caro, both for what she'd lost and for what should have been. Her parents had been gone five years, the victims of a car accident. She'd been the one to positively identify their bodies, yet she still sometimes found herself reaching for the telephone to call them.

If she were looking for an excuse as to why she'd married Truman, that would be it. She'd been so lonely, so very lost after their deaths. And he'd been understanding and supportive. He'd taken charge, helped her make decisions when she was too grief-stricken to do so. It wasn't until later she'd realized how controlling he could be.

She forced herself back to the matter at hand. She was relieved that she wouldn't be spending the night alone in the ramshackle inn with its brooding owner, but now she felt like an intruder. Quite obviously, this was a family gathering and she was an outsider. It didn't help that all eyes were on her when she and Jake stepped into the room. The older man glanced up from his book, the children stopped playing and the couple on the couch shifted to sitting positions.

One of the children was the first to break the silence.

"Uncle Jake's back! Uncle Jake's back!" squealed the little girl. She hopped up and shot across the floor to wrap one of his legs in an embrace.

Not to be outdone, the little boy followed suit. He didn't just hug Jake's leg, he tried to scale it. Caro smiled. It was just the sort of thing Cabot would do. Jake's reaction, however, was the polar opposite of what

Truman's would have been. Instead of being befuddled by the boy's exuberance and a little embarrassed by the affectionate display, Jake scooped him up in his arms.

"Hey, munchkin."

Caro's heart did a strange *thunk-thunk,* which she attributed to wishing for what already should have been the case for her son: a father who not only enjoyed his silly antics but would take part in them. It had nothing to do with Jake, even if at the moment he seemed nothing like the brooding man who not so long ago had begrudgingly offered her shelter from the storm.

His smile was real, smoky blue eyes alight with teasing humor. He was all the more handsome for it.

Thunk, thunk!

This time Caro outright ignored the sensation.

"Daddy said you were going to freeze your fool head off out in the snow."

Leave it to a child to rat out an adult. But she wisely hid her smile. And good thing, too, since right after Jake asked in an amused voice, "Did he now?" he shot a dark look in the direction of the couch, where the man in question sat, hands on his knees and ready to rise.

Brothers, she decided, and felt another bubble of envy swell. Caro was an only child.

The little boy grinned and nodded vigorously. "Yep. But Grandpa said that a little time alone would do you good." Now he frowned. "Did it?"

Half of Jake's mouth rose. "For the most part."

"Well, I'm glad you're back, Uncle Jake," the little girl enthused. "Mommy and Grandma were getting worried that something had happened."

"What about you?" Jake asked.

"A little. But you're in-in…" She scrunched up her pretty little face and glanced toward the couch. "What's that word from the superhero movie we watched last week, Daddy?"

"Invincible," the man supplied. His lips twisted on the word.

The child repeated it with an adorable lisp while Jake's expression turned rueful.

His gaze was on his brother when he said, "I'm no hero, super or otherwise."

He set both of the kids down, even as the

couple on the couch and the older man in the rocker rose and stepped forward.

Caro sensed a second meaning to Jake's words that made her curious, but she didn't comment on it. She was a guest, one even less welcome than his family apparently was. The underlying tension here was impossible to miss.

No matter, she assured herself. She would be on her way as soon as the snow slowed down and a wrecker could pull out her car.

Which reminded her. "Excuse me, can I use your telephone?"

Before Jake could answer, the little boy asked, "Who's this, Uncle Jake?"

She didn't wait to be introduced. "I'm Caro. Your uncle may not be a superhero, but he did rescue me from the storm. My car got stuck in a drift."

It was a little bit more than stuck, but she mentally crossed her fingers that whatever damage the front had sustained could be repaired without too much fuss.

Jake glanced sharply in her direction. An odd mix of anger and bewilderment colored his expression.

"Right place, right time," he mumbled. He was back to the surly man who'd first stumbled across her, leaving her to wonder what she'd said to irritate him.

"I'm Jillian," the little girl said. She stuck out her hand, which Caro shook. "I'm six and I have a loose tooth. Want to see?"

Without waiting for a reply, Jillian opened her mouth and used the tip of her tongue to wiggle one of her top front teeth. Her already-adorable lisp was going to become even more pronounced soon, Caro thought.

"Jilly," reprimanded the woman from the couch, who was now, along with the man Caro assumed was Jake's brother and the older man, gathered around Caro in a semi-circle, smiling politely even as they stared openly. "Sorry about that."

"That's all right. A loose tooth is pretty exciting news for a child."

Jake cleared his throat and apparently remembered his manners. "Caro, this is my sister-in-law, Bonnie, and my brother, Dean. You've met Jillian, of course. Her brother is Riley."

"I'm almost five," Riley informed Caro, holding up the corresponding number of digits.

Jillian rolled her eyes. "He just turned four last week."

Only children were so eager to add a year to their age. Caro bent down to shake his hand. "It's nice to meet you, Riley."

The boy's wide grin revealed a pair of dimples that melted Caro's heart. Cabot had dimples.

"And this is my father, Martin McCabe," Jake was saying.

"It's nice to meet you, Mr. McCabe." Her hand was swallowed up in one of Martin's giant paws.

"Likewise."

Doreen returned then with a couple of towels, making Caro aware of how bedraggled she must look. Truman and his mother would be appalled that she was standing in a roomful of strangers looking like something the cat had dragged in. But then the Wendells wouldn't socialize with people like the McCabes in the first place. Unless she missed her guess, they weren't blue-blooded snobs who sat around at dry dinner parties discussing investment strategies, mutual funds and which couples in their social class had failed to make a killing in the stock market.

The McCabes, she realized, were more

like her parents had been, down-to-earth folks who valued family, God and country.

The old ache throbbed to life a second time, a little more pronounced. She wrapped her arms about herself, seeking comfort she knew from experience wouldn't come.

"Good heavens, child! You're shaking. Get closer to the fire," Doreen instructed.

"I'm fine," Caro began. Her protest was lost as the older woman began issuing orders.

"Martin, throw another log on the fire. Dean, give the poor girl the afghan from the couch." She eyed Caro a moment before continuing. "Bonnie should have something to fit you even though you're a bit taller." The older woman's lips pursed. "And a little on the thin side."

"Oh, that's all right. I don't want to be a bother."

"Then what were you thinking heading out in a snowstorm?" Jake demanded.

His mother gasped, presumably at his rude question and not-so-nice tone. It was his tone, as much as his words, that caused Caro's spine to straighten. Her hands dropped to her sides where her hands fisted.

"I have somewhere I need to be."

"Not in a storm, you don't."

"Jacob!"

They both ignored Doreen's shout.

"Storm or no storm, it's important."

"Nothing is *that* important," he drawled. "Trust me."

"This is." Thinking of Cabot and Truman's stipulations, Caro swallowed a sob. It wouldn't do to fall apart now. "I have…a deadline to meet."

"Work?" He snorted in disgust. "You risked your life for work?"

Let him think what he would. "Unlike you, I wasn't out in a blizzard to ride a horse."

She felt exhilarated, having given as good as she'd got. Meekness no longer suited her. In truth, it never had. But numb as she'd been for four years, first from grief and later from disbelief, she'd fallen into the ill-fitting role. God help her, she would don it again if need be.

That thought had her sobering.

Jake gaped at her, his wide mouth going slack for just a second before his lips pressed together in a flat line. She heard Dean's muffled laughter and a glance around confirmed that the rest of the McCabe clan found her dressing-down of one of their members amusing rather than in poor taste. Even so,

Caro was appalled. Whether the man had it coming or not, she was being unforgivably rude.

"I'm sorry. I…I…"

Jake unclamped his jaw just enough to say, "You mentioned something earlier about needing to make a phone call."

"Yes. My cell's not picking up a signal."

"Follow me."

Doreen settled the afghan around Caro's shoulders. "Don't worry," she whispered. "My son's bark is a lot worse than his bite."

Not quite sure what to make of that assessment, Caro offered a weak smile.

Jake was waiting for her at the tall reception desk near the front entrance. A small brass lamp with an oblong shade lit a guest book that was yellowed from age. The telephone, an ancient-looking thing with a twisted cord, rotary dial and clunky black receiver, was next to it.

"It's not a local call," she said.

"Fine." He pushed the telephone toward her.

"I'll reimburse you for the charges." It looked as if he could use the money, given the state of the inn. It was a shame, too. The place had such great potential. That much was obvious despite its disrepair.

"Just make your call."

Jake stomped away. He was angry, but not at Caro, even if he thought she should have stayed tucked safe in her home rather than venturing out in foul weather.

For work!

But the person he was good and angry at was himself. He was angry with the way he was acting. Angry with Dean that his younger brother had called him out on his self-prescribed isolation and stirred up emotions that had only recently begun to settle.

"You're being selfish," Dean had said earlier that day.

Jake's family had arrived en masse the evening before, showing up at his doorstep, all grins and giggles, in an SUV they'd rented after touching down at the airport in Montpelier.

"I just want to be left alone."

"No, you just want to stew. You got screwed, bro. No two ways about it. They set you up to take a fall. You took it." The younger man set his hands on his hips and shook his head. "I never understood that."

"A woman was dead. Her child, too. A colleague killed himself afterward."

And then, Miranda...

"But it wasn't your fault. You didn't get the address wrong," Dean had insisted. "Someone as anal as you doesn't get stuff like that wrong."

Jake wanted to believe it, but he couldn't be sure. Not anymore. Not without proof. "I was in charge. It happened on my watch, which makes it my fault."

All of it.

"So you keep saying. But it's been more than a year. When are you going to cut yourself some slack and rejoin the land of the living?"

The woman and her child didn't have that luxury. Nor did the rookie cop. Those were facts he couldn't move beyond. Between them and the media scrutiny his family had endured, and his wife's decision not only to divorce him but to abort their child, going into exile had seemed the only solution.

"There's nothing for me back there."

"Except your family."

The words hit with the impact of flaming arrows, which was Dean's intention. Jake missed his parents. As annoying as Dean could be, he missed his brother, too. And then there were Bonnie and the kids. They were a tight-knit family.

"You know what I mean."

"Yeah. I know." His brother had snorted. "So, you're in Vermont to make a fresh start?"

Jake had said nothing.

"That's what I thought. If I believed you really wanted to be here, that would be different. But you're here basically hiding out," he accused a second time. "And while you're busy with your pity party, Mom and Dad are left hurting, and my kids are left to wonder why their uncle moved to another state and is living like a hermit."

"You don't get it," Jake had snapped. "I did this for you. I did this for *all* of you."

"No, bro. We can take care of ourselves. You did this for yourself. You did this because, in addition to the nasty fallout from that unfortunate police raid, you can't face what Miranda did."

Jake had grabbed his brother by the shirt. The old rage boiled inside him, tempting him to take a swing. Instead, he'd let Dean loose, found his coat and headed out into the storm. His temper had yet to subside when he'd spied Caro through the falling snow.

He glanced at her now from the door that led to the kitchen. He couldn't hear what she was saying into the telephone receiver, but she wasn't happy. The rigid set of her shoulders and the down-turned corners of her mouth said as much.

What was her story?

There was more to it than she claimed, of that Jake was sure. He might no longer be a cop, but his instincts when it came to people were still good. She didn't fit the portrait of a driven career woman. Something about her was too soft for the hard-edged, high-stakes business world. And the quality of her clothes screamed high society, even if her car had screamed penny-pincher. Yet she'd endangered her life to meet a deadline.

Why?

She said it was important. Something illegal? His gut told him no, but Jake couldn't shake his first impression that she was desperate.

Not my problem, he reminded himself, putting his curiosity aside. It was back in an instant when her expression softened and her lips curved into a smile.

Just who was on the other end of the line to make her scowl one moment and melt like butter the next?

She twirled the phone cord around the fingers on her left hand as she spoke. No rings that he could see, but the conversation she was having now had nothing to do with business.

I love you.

Jake didn't hear the words. Rather, he saw her lips form them just before she set the receiver back in its cradle. He wasn't disappointed that she was involved with someone, even if he did find her attractive. He was past all but the most primal of feelings where women were concerned. He had his ex-wife to thank for that. Besides, he barely knew this woman. Caro hadn't deceived him. She hadn't betrayed him. She hadn't had time to offer more than cursory explanations.

If she had, would she?

He realized he was still staring at her, probably with a scowl on his face, given her startled expression when she spied him. Her eyebrows lifted; her lips parted. He let loose a mild expletive as he levered away from the doorjamb.

Jake never had been the life of the party.

That was Dean with his easy smile and open demeanor. But these days Jake knew he came off as unapproachable. Only his family was immune to his black moods and foul temper.

And this woman, apparently.

Caro surprised him by crossing to where he stood.

He said the first thing that came to mind. "Did you get through okay?"

"Yes, thanks."

"Crisis averted?"

A shadow crept over her face. "What do you mean?"

"The deadline you spoke of. Did you get an extension or a reprieve or…whatever?"

She nodded. "Sort of. For now."

Why didn't she look happy about it? A moment ago she'd been smiling and whispering words of love to the party on the other end of the line.

"That's a good thing, right?"

"Right." It was said for his benefit, as was the smile that lifted the corners of her mouth. Her eyes were saying something else. It wasn't desperation he saw in them now. Not entirely, at least. He spied apprehension, nerves. That delayed deadline?

More questions bubbled. After all, it was Saturday afternoon. Tomorrow was Easter Sunday. Just what kind of work was she involved in that required her to be on the clock over a holiday weekend?

And then there was the way she'd ended the phone call. Perhaps she'd had a spat with her lover and they'd resolved it over the phone, but now she was stranded and they wouldn't be together for the weekend.

That was it, he decided.

"He must be special."

"Very." She sighed, and then flushed. "Wh-who?"

Case closed. "Never mind."

"I also need to call a garage for a wrecker. I wonder if you might have a telephone directory?"

He found a dog-eared book in one of the drawers at the registration desk. It was outdated by half a dozen years. Caro frowned when he handed it to her.

"You don't have anything more recent?"

"No, but I doubt it will matter. The town hasn't changed much in the past three decades."

Quaint, old-fashioned, it was the same year after year. That was part of its draw for tourists. That was exactly its draw for Jake now. He needed a place where his memories weren't tainted with the stain of the events back in Buffalo.

"Do you have a recommendation?"

He scratched his chin, thinking. "Try Orville's. They do towing as well as repairs, and it looks like you might have some damage."

This time, he left her alone to make the call, returning to the living room where his family waited. It was a bad choice if he'd hoped to avoid confrontation. His mother spoke first, which wasn't surprising. His father preferred to stay in the background, asserting himself only when necessary, but then to great effect. Martin McCabe might be a quiet man, but he was no pushover. Still waters, according to Doreen. And she claimed that, of her two sons, Jake was the one who had inherited the quality.

"Who is she?"

"Just a woman who had the bad luck to have her car go off the road in a storm."

"A good-looking woman," Dean mumbled, earning a smack on the arm from his wife.

"Where is she from?"

"Where is she heading?"

"Where is she now?"

His family pelted him with questions. Jake answered his mother's first.

"She's calling for a tow truck. I told her to try Orville's"

"Is he still in business?" his father asked.

"Apparently."

"Do you really think he will come out in this weather?" Dean wanted to know.

"Not likely."

"Which means she'll be spending the night here." Doreen clicked her tongue. "Heavens, I'd better get busy cleaning up another guest room. God knows they're not habitable in their present condition."

"I'll give you a hand," Bonnie offered.

They started toward the door.

"There's no need. Caro can have mine," Jake said.

The chivalrous gesture had his mother smiling and nodding. His brother's grin, however, had Jake clarifying, "I'll sleep on the couch in here."

"Can I sleep down here with Uncle Jake?" Riley wanted to know. He danced excitedly in a circle.

"Me, too! Me, too!" Jillian chanted.

"You'll sleep upstairs with us," Bonnie

said. Before they could protest, she added, "Remember, the Easter Bunny is coming tonight. It wouldn't do for him to stumble over a couple of sleeping children while trying to hide your baskets full of treats."

That quieted them, but only for a moment.

"When are we going to color the eggs?" Jillian asked, hopping on one foot.

"Let's do it now!" Riley squealed.

"After dinner and before bath time," their mother said.

On their way from Montpelier's airport, they'd stopped at a grocery store. They had everything for the holiday feast with them, from the eggs the children were itching to dye to the honey-glazed ham that would be served the following day for dinner. Doreen even had packed the fancy Irish linens the McCabes used every holiday. Jake took in the scene before him. The kids scampering about, his father smoking a pipe while seated fireside. It was so damned easy to pretend that everything was the same with his family here.

Except that it wasn't. Nothing was the same. This family gathering was different. Someone was missing…and he didn't mean his ex-wife.

He glanced toward the doorway. Caro stood there—looking tentative, looking utterly beautiful despite her damp hair and pinched expression. She was nothing like Miranda, despite their shared affinity for high-quality clothing. Miranda's features were far sharper. The description he kept coming back to when it came to this woman was soft, fragile.

Jake cleared his throat. "Any luck getting a tow truck to come out?"

"No. A man answered at the place you suggested, but he said the roads were impassable and he had a dozen or so requests for assistance to handle ahead of mine. With tomorrow being a holiday, he said it would be Monday at the earliest before he could tow my car to his garage."

Some of that desperation leaked back into her expression. "Is there another garage I should try?"

"Maybe. But I have a feeling they'd all tell you the same thing," Jake replied.

She nodded glumly.

"Well, not to worry. You're welcome here," Doreen said. "You'll take Jake's room."

Her eyelids flickered. In surprise or dismay? "Oh, no. I couldn't—"

"He insists," Doreen said.

At Caro's dubious expression, Jake added, "Actually, I do. It will save my mother and Bonnie from having to clean up another one of the guest rooms."

She smiled. "Well, in that case..."

"You'd probably like a hot shower," Doreen said. "Show her where everything is, Jake, while Bonnie and I try to come up with a change of clothes."

Having been given his marching orders, Jake headed for the stairs. Even though Caro was behind him, he swore he could smell the subtle, sexy scent that wafted from her person.

CHAPTER THREE

CARO FOLLOWED JAKE UP the stairs just past the reception desk. The oak banister wobbled under her hand and the steps creaked beneath a maroon carpet runner that was worn and faded from age.

At the top, he turned right, bypassing two doors before stopping to open the third.

"This is it," he said.

Jake stepped backward to allow her to enter the room first. She'd assumed she would follow him inside and so they wound up bumping into one another. The side of his foot came down on her big toe and the point of his elbow found her breast.

"God, sorry."

"Excuse me," she said.

Their words were issued simultaneously and with an equal measure of awkwardness.

"Um, are you…okay?" he asked.

"Fine. Good thing you aren't still wearing your boots." Caro chose to ignore entirely the other injury she'd suffered.

This time she was ready when Jake waved her ahead.

The room was a good size, with a dormer wide enough to fit a desk and a sitting area comprised of two wingback chairs that flanked a fireplace. Clothes were draped over the chairs, making it clear sitting wasn't their function these days. But the fireplace looked to be in working order, if the ashes and charred log inside the opening were any indication.

Caro wished it were lit now. She felt as if she would never be warm again. But she didn't ask Jake to indulge her. She'd put him through too much trouble already.

The other main focus of the room, of course, was the bed. It was an antique brass number that she'd bet was original to the inn. She crossed to get a better look at the detail work on the tarnished headboard. As she rested one hand on the cool metal, the covers distracted her. They lay in a twisted heap in the center of the sagging mattress. Hers always looked the same by morning, no matter how diligently she tucked in the sheets.

She pictured Jake there, tossing and turning. Intrigued, she nonetheless forced the image away.

He cleared his throat, making her aware that he stood just behind her. Caro turned. She could only imagine what he was thinking.

"You're a restless sleeper," she said inanely.

His brows shot up.

"The covers." She motioned to them with one hand. "They're all bunched up."

"I would have straightened my bed if I'd known someone besides me would be sleeping in it tonight. I wasn't expecting company. More company, that is."

"I didn't mean to sound critical," she offered hastily. "In fact, my covers always look the same by morning."

His brows rose again, making her feel foolish and flustered. She didn't care for either sensation. So, when she spoke again, her tone was no-nonsense. "Anyway, I really do appreciate your giving up your bed for me. The room is very nice. Lovely in fact."

His laughter startled her almost as much as the transformation humor made on his appearance.

"It's a dump, Caro. The whole place is."

He sobered then as he glanced around. "It wasn't always like this and it won't be by the time I'm finished. I'll make it right."

She wasn't sure how to respond to that final fierce declaration. In the end, it didn't matter. He switched gears and returned to more practical matters.

"There are only three bathrooms that are in working order in the entire place. One is on the main floor next to what used to be the caretaker's quarters. The other two are up here, including the one through there." He pointed to a door on the far side of the room. "Sorry I wasn't able to go back for your bag, but you'll find most of the basics—soap, shampoo, toothpaste. I think there's even a new toothbrush in one of the vanity drawers."

"Thanks. I'm sure I'll be fine." She offered a smile. "It sure beats sleeping in a snowdrift."

"You wouldn't be sleeping. You'd be dead."

Her smile vanished.

"Sorry." He glanced away.

For the first time, she noticed a small, crescent-shaped scar at the corner of his left eye. She had one similar in size and shape on the underside of her chin, the result of a fall off her bike when she was six. Truman considered it a defect and had tried more than once to talk her into seeing a plastic surgeon to have it made less noticeable.

She was glad she'd resisted. As it was, he'd managed to erase so much of her personality and her person, remaking her into an image she'd barely recognized when she gazed in the mirror. One of the first things she'd done after leaving him was to dye her hair back to something resembling its natural shade of caramel-brown. He'd preferred her as a blonde, and he knew best, after all.

"Sorry," Jake said again, pulling her from her musings. This time he sounded a little more irritated than contrite.

"No need to apologize. Besides, you're right. I was already in serious trouble when you happened along," Caro admitted. "And I didn't mean to stare at you just now. It's just that I was noticing your scar."

On impulse she reached over and traced its smooth surface with one fingertip. He pulled backward as if she'd struck him.

"It gives your face character."

"That's putting it politely." He didn't sound convinced. Nor did he appear to appreciate her forwardness.

"I have one, too." She tilted up her chin and pointed. "See? Right here."

He cupped the side of her face and turned her head slightly to get a better look. His callused hand felt rough against her skin. She told herself that was the only reason for the odd sensation his touch inspired.

"How'd you get yours?" he asked as he withdrew his hand.

"I fell off my bike and hit the handlebars on my way down. I was six. You?"

"Eleven. Dean and I were horsing around and I took a header off the front porch. My mother's stone birdbath broke my fall." He rubbed his temple. "I wound up with a concussion and we both wound up grounded."

"That doesn't seem fair."

"I was older." He shrugged. "Supposedly, I knew better."

"Hi." Bonnie knocked at the opened door before entering. "I come bearing clothes. Sorry to say, all I have for you is a robe and a pair of wool socks. I didn't bring a second pair of pajamas."

"There's no need to apologize. I really appreciate this."

Caro took the berry-colored terry-cloth robe from Bonnie's hands. It was soft and looked warm, as did the gray socks. That was all that mattered.

"Aren't you going to light the fireplace, Jake?" Bonnie asked.

Caro could have hugged her.

"I guess I could," he said slowly.

"It would help take the chill off," Bonnie said, sending Caro a grin.

"The inn's furnace needs to be replaced. It's on my to-do list." He sighed then. "Along with a lot of other things."

"Dean's told me stories about this place. He said it was something else when you were kids. He remembers the two of you playing hide-and-seek in the common rooms and sliding down the banister."

Jake grunted. "The banister couldn't take Riley's weight now without splintering into pieces."

"He's getting big." Unless Caro missed her guess, Bonnie was purposely misunderstanding his meaning. "Doreen says he's the spitting image of Dean at that age. He's all McCabe. Same with Jillian."

A muscle ticked in Jake's jaw and something akin to pain flashed in his eyes.

The silence stretched. Before it could become too awkward, though, Bonnie dusted her hands together.

"Well, just to let you know, Mom's reheating the pot of five-alarm chili she made earlier. She told me to tell you it would be ready whenever you and Caro are hungry."

Caro's stomach growled as if on command, making her realize she was all but starving. The piece of toast and cup of tea she'd had several hours earlier had barely been enough to sustain her through the morning. Adrenaline, however, had staved off the worst of her hunger.

Apparently, until just now.

Caro wanted to be appalled. She found herself laughing out loud instead. Bonnie joined in. Jake, however, gaped as if she'd gone mad.

In her head, Caro heard her mother-in-law say sternly: "Only a woman of ill breeding would comport herself in such a manner."

Caro sobered.

"What about you guys?" Jake was asking Bonnie.

"Oh, we ate a little over an hour ago."

"Jillian said you were worried about me," he reminded her wryly.

"I was, which is why I indulged in two

bowls." Bonnie's smile vanished and she poked his chest with her index finger. "Don't do that again. I don't care how much Dean ticks you off. Don't do that again. Do you hear me?"

Jake grabbed hold of the finger before she could jab him a second time and gave it a squeeze. "I hear you. Next time, I'll pick Dean up and dump him outside in the snow."

"One stipulation," she said.

"Anything."

"Wait until I have the camera handy." Bonnie left the room chuckling.

"That's nice."

Jake turned to face Caro. "What?"

"You, your family. It's obvious that you're all very close."

He nodded, but from his expression it was hard to tell if he was happy about that.

"You're lucky," she murmured, thinking about her own parents and the bond they'd shared.

Caro hugged the robe to her chest. God, she missed them. She missed their frequent phone calls, their encouragement, their support. She even missed their counsel, which had bordered on meddling at times, but it had always been well-intentioned. They'd loved her. Unconditionally. Only one person in the whole world loved Caro that way now. Cabot. She couldn't lose him to Truman and allow his sweet, open nature to be corrupted by the Wendells' strict code of behavior.

"Go take your shower."

Jake's gruffly issued words snapped her back to the present.

"I won't be long," she promised. Before she could close the bathroom door, his voice stopped her.

"Caro?"

"Yes?"

He was frowning again, but he didn't appear angry. Concerned? She decided she must have imagined that because in the end all he said was, "Don't use all the hot water."

Jake scrubbed a hand over his face after the door closed behind Caro. For just a moment, she'd looked so lost and vulnerable. He'd wanted to ask her what was troubling her. It wasn't his concern, he reminded himself again. He was out of the hero business, done with trying to save or change lives. If he'd truly suffered from the God Complex some people had accused him of, he was over it now. Cured for good. He hadn't been able to help his own unborn child.

He heard Caro turn on the water. The taps squeaked in protest and the pipes knocked together. As he made his way to the closet, Jake mentally added both to that long list of repairs that included the banister. He found a pair of jeans and a thick black sweater. Although he'd told Caro to save him some hot water, his shower could wait. He changed quickly and went downstairs. When he returned with an armful of logs and some kindling a few minutes later, the water was still running and he thought he could hear her humming. By the time it switched off, the kindling was aflame and he was adding the first log.

"Oh."

Caro stopped in the threshold, clearly not expecting to find him kneeling in front of the hearth. Steam floated out around her as she stood framed in the door. She hastily gathered the robe together. Nearly every inch of her was covered now, including her feet, thanks to Bonnie's wool socks.

How was it possible that she still looked sexy?

Maybe it was because he'd glimpsed a

pink bra and equally delicate-looking pair of panties before she managed to secure the robe.

He forced himself to forget about silk and lace and concentrate on the damp wool pants and turtleneck sweater that were draped over her arm.

"I got a fire going for you."

"Thank you."

She brought her free hand up and ran her fingers through the length of her wet hair. The gesture bespoke nerves rather than flirting, but his libido didn't care about the distinction. Interest welled up as she pushed a tangle of curls back from her face. Even without a stitch of makeup, she was lovely, ivory skin all but translucent in the light from the bedside lamp and the subtler glow of firelight.

It looked soft, too. The kind of skin a man wanted to take his time running his hands over.

He ran his hands over his whisker-roughened face instead and pushed to his feet, uncomfortable not only with the direction of his thoughts but his seeming inability to control them.

"I'll get out of your way."

"I...I saved you some hot water," she said as he started for the door.

"Thanks, but I decided I'd eat first. My stomach doesn't want to wait."

He stopped to pick up his wet clothes, and chanced a glance back at her. It was the wrong thing to do. She was nibbling her bottom lip, a task he would be only too happy to do for her.

"I can take your wet clothes," he forced himself to say. His manners might be rusty, but they weren't lacking entirely, especially with his mother on hand and eager to remind him how civilized people acted around company. "The inn has a laundry room."

"These are dry-clean only."

Of course they were. "My mom will know what to do with them."

"Oh. Well, then, terrific." She handed them over. "I'll be down in a minute. I just want to blow-dry my hair first."

Caro was as good as her word. She padded softly into the kitchen as Jake sat at the table spooning up chili. His mother was fussing at the sink, washing the bowls, cups and utensils the rest of his family had used earlier. Doreen wiped her hands on a towel and smiled warmly. If there was one thing his mother could be counted on to do, it was to make guests, even unexpected ones, feel welcome.

"Don't you look all refreshed and pretty now," she enthused. Before Caro could answer, Doreen was already shooing her toward the table. "Go and sit and I'll get you a bowl of chili. It will warm you up from the inside the same way the shower warmed you up from the outside."

Caro took the seat opposite Jake's. Her gaze stayed on his only a moment before it strayed to the window.

"I can't believe this weather," she murmured. "It's Easter weekend."

Outside, the snow had yet to let up. In fact, it was coming down as hard as ever in the same huge flakes.

If Dean hadn't ticked him off, and Jake hadn't stalked out to work off his temper, Caro might still be waiting for help. All alone. Freezing. Her gaze was back on his. Something in her expression told him she was thinking the same thing. Any second now she would be thanking him again. The last thing Jake wanted was more gratitude.

"Yeah, well, a good nor'easter doesn't give a damn about the calendar," Jake said.

"Language," Doreen admonished as she set a steaming bowl of spicy soup in front of Caro. "The local forecast is calling for another four inches before it begins to taper off this evening."

"There must be a good foot out there already," Caro remarked.

Growing up in North Carolina, she had never gotten used to snow. At least not this much of it. Even several years in New England hadn't prepared her for a late storm of this magnitude.

"At this rate, it's going to take road crews a couple of days to make the main roads passable," Doreen said. She sent a wink in her son's direction. "It's a good thing we were planning to make it a long weekend anyway."

Jake ignored her. "Don't worry. I imagine the interstate will be among the first roads plowed," he told Caro.

She nodded and picked up her spoon. "Well, once I get where I need to be, it can snow until June for all I care."

The kids rushed into the kitchen then, once again clamoring to dye eggs.

"Please, Grammy," Jillian begged in her high-pitched voice.

"Pretty please with a cherry on top," Riley added, not to be outdone.

Doreen ushered them out, presumably in search of their mother to get the okay. Jake's attention stayed on Caro. She certainly was determined to get where she needed to be, he thought again. All because of some man? His cop instincts were telling him no, but then he'd been in love once. He knew firsthand how much the emotion could blind someone to reality.

"Word to the wise," he began. His gruff tone startled Caro, who flinched. He decided not only to moderate his tone, but to change what he'd been about to say. He pointed to her bowl with the business end of his spoon. "My mother's chili is known for its heat."

CHAPTER FOUR

EVENING BEGAN TO FALL before Caro was ready for it. All things considered, she was having a decent time. An interesting time, she amended as she spied Jake.

He was seated with Dean at the small table on the other side of the living room from where she sat on the couch with his mother and sister-in-law. The men were playing chess, a game Caro knew from experience required both skill and concentration to win. Unless she missed her guess, he was three moves from checkmate. Yet every time she glanced over, his gaze was on her, those deep-set blue eyes full of questions and not nearly enough answers for her liking.

He made her feel vulnerable and oddly exposed, which perhaps explained why her hands always went to the lapels of her robe afterward, as if to ensure her modesty.

After eating Doreen's chili, which had been every bit as spicy as Jake warned, Caro had considered going back upstairs. But to do what? Sit in a room by herself and fret as she stared out at the falling snow? She was in the mood to be around people. So, instead, she'd remained downstairs. Jake's family made her feel welcomed.

She'd nearly forgotten what it was like to be so at ease—and while wearing a borrowed bathrobe, her hair a mess and her makeup long gone, no less.

Truman's mother had found fault with everything from the moment her son proposed. Truman, too, was critical, but he'd claimed his criticism was intended for her betterment and to help her fit in with his social circle.

You're a diamond in the rough, Caroline. With the right clothes and a little polish, you'll outshine all others.

Her initial flattery over his assessment gave way to frustration, then exasperation and finally irritation. She wasn't a lump of clay to be molded, as malleable as she must have seemed when they first met. When she found her backbone, the arguments began. She might have left him, but she was old-fashioned enough to want to try to honor her vows, to find a common ground, especially when she discovered she was pregnant.

Then along came Cabot, and despite the harried pace of new parenthood things seemed to fall into place. Even if theirs would never be a great love match, she and Truman were no longer at odds. He respected Caro's decisions and trusted her judgment where their son was concerned.

Unless his mother was around.

Unfortunately, Susan's visits became more and more frequent as time went on, and just after Cabot's first birthday, she moved into their home. She did so with Truman's blessing and without Caro's consent or much prior knowledge, for that matter.

As soon as Susan Wendell settled into the guest wing of their home, Caro's tiny island of contentment began to erode. Not even the joy she found in motherhood was enough to offset her growing unhappiness.

It didn't help matters that her mother-in-law increasingly usurped Caro's role as both Cabot's mother and the woman of the house. Dinner menus, social functions, Cabot's bedtime, even the new furniture for the great room—all bore Susan's stamp. And any time Caro complained to Truman in private or spoke up in front of Susan, she was made out to be spiteful or ungrateful.

She's just trying to help, Caroline.

How many times had she heard that?

She'd gritted her teeth and tried to make it work, going along to get along for the sake of her son. Until one day she knew she could take no more.

The final straw hadn't been something big. Nothing dramatic happened. There'd been no heated arguments. No lines drawn in the sand. Rather, Caro was watching as her son played at the park. Other children were in the sandbox, best friends after having just met mere minutes earlier. But Cabot stood away from them, looking uncertain and looking like an outsider dressed as he was per Susan Wendell's specifications: no denim and no pullover shirts. He was wearing belted tan walking shorts and a collared blue button-down. Both were designer label, of course.

At three years old, the boy owned more starched oxfords, bow ties and blazers than most adult male professionals. He was a miniature version of his father, becoming more so by the day, and in ways far more concerning than his clothing.

That had been Caro's wake-up call.

She did not want to raise another Truman Wendell. She did not want to raise a son who would be entrenched in and trapped by convention, roles and rules. She didn't want to raise a son who would expect perfection at the expense of his own contentment. Or who would manipulate others even as he allowed himself to be manipulated, as Truman did with his mother.

She wanted Cabot to be a toddler boy, not a miniature man. She wanted him to laugh often and maybe just a bit too loudly, as Riley and Jillian were doing now across the room. The children had changed into their pajamas and were sharing space on their grandfather's lap as he read them a bedtime story.

A couple of hours earlier, they'd colored eggs, insisting that Caro join them. She glanced down at her hands. The tips of her fingers were an unidentifiable shade, but that was a small price to pay for the fun she'd had.

"That will come off eventually, you know," Bonnie said to her now.

"Oh, I know."

"You should have used the spoon to lift the eggs out of the coloring," Bonnie replied, though the tips of her own fingers were similarly hued.

"But where's the fun in that?"

"Exactly."

Caro had planned to enjoy this Easter tradition with Cabot. Just as she'd planned for him to wake in the morning in their small apartment and have to hunt for a basket filled with treats and other goodies before they dressed and headed to church.

None of that was to be.

Instead, her son would wake in the big house on Lake Champlain to find a basket the size of a small car brimming with more toys than most children received for their birthday and Christmas combined.

From past experience, Caro knew that regardless of what she had picked for him to wear, he would be outfitted in a little suit with a pastel shirt and striped tie that coordinated with Truman's. Susan would see to it. Then he would be bustled off to church before he could snatch so much as a jelly bean from his basket.

Once there, he would be marched up the main aisle of the church the Wendell family had attended since before the turn of the last century. He would sit in the pew that no other family dared to lay claim to even on those Sundays when the Wendells were out of town.

And Susan would be beside him, tapping his head when he became too fidgety, which would be almost immediately. He was three, after all.

Caro glanced up and found herself lost in a pair of questioning blue eyes. But only for a moment. Jake's gaze was still on her when he said, "Checkmate."

Pushing back his chair, he stood, and, even as Dean sputtered in protest, he took his leave.

She couldn't quite figure him out. One minute he seemed the epitome of a loner: gruff and uncommunicative. The next, the sort who put family before all else.

"You're frowning, dear." Doreen made this assessment as she sipped her coffee. "Is everything all right."

Caro blinked. "My mind wandered. Sorry."

"No need to apologize for that." Doreen, however, wasn't fooled. "Are you missing your family?"

Caro swallowed.

"My...my family?" To her horror, her eyes misted with tears. Perhaps it was the events of the day or the fact that her separation from her son was being extended due to circumstances beyond her control, but yes, she was indeed missing her family. The parents she'd lost all too tragically and the little boy who was all she had left in the world.

She couldn't bear to lose him, too.

"I'm sorry." Doreen was the one to apologize this time. She reached over to rest a comforting hand on Caro's arm. "I didn't mean to upset you. Of course you're missing your family. It's Easter. It's always hard to be away from loved ones on holidays."

"That's why we're here," Bonnie chimed in. "To be with Jake."

Dean sauntered over then. "That's right. My brother wouldn't come to us, so we came to him in Vermont."

"It wasn't so much he wouldn't," Doreen inserted. "He just…couldn't."

Caro was curious, but she didn't want to pry, especially if Jake were around to hear her. She glanced toward the door. When she didn't see him, she asked, "The inn?"

"Among other things," his mother said slowly. "He recently came through a bad spell."

"He was screwed over, Mom. And instead of fighting back, he decided to take it."

"Language, Dean."

"Sorry, but let's call a spade a spade. The department hung him out to dry. And then Miranda...God, what she did to him." Shaking his head, he stalked away.

"You'll have to excuse him," Bonnie said once her husband was gone. "Dean has strong opinions and he doesn't know when to keep them to himself, which is why Jake was out in the storm in the first place. We hadn't been here twenty-four hours and already Dean had started in on him."

"It's a family trait, I'm afraid," Doreen said. With a wink, she added, "On their father's side."

Screwed over? How? Dean had started in on Jake about what? And who was this Miranda and just what had she done? Far from being satisfied, Caro's curiosity kicked into overdrive.

But the only question she deemed polite enough to ask was, "How long has he owned the inn?"

"About six months now," Doreen said.

"Has he always wanted to be an inn-keeper?"

"Good heavens, no." The older woman chuckled. "We were as surprised as anyone when he called to say he'd bought the old place." She glanced around now and sighed. "Although it was something back in the day."

"It needs a lot of tender loving care to be restored, but Jake's just the person to do it." This from Bonnie, who added, "And it will keep his mind off...things."

"What do you do for a living?" Doreen asked, more likely in an effort to change the subject than out of actual interest.

"I'm a guidance counselor." Or Caro had been, for one of the most prestigious prep schools in Vermont. These days, with the economy being what it was, she'd been lucky to find a part-time position in a public school district. It paid a quarter of her previous salary, but she wasn't complaining. It was work, she needed the money and the kids made it worthwhile. Kids always did.

"Are you from around here?"

She shook her head. "I was just passing through today. I live in a small town south of Montpelier."

"Is that where your parents live?" Bonnie asked innocently.

Caro's heart squeezed. "No. They lived in North Carolina. They're...gone now. Both of them. In an automobile accident five years this spring."

Caro stared into her coffee mug now as more tears gathered and threatened to fall. These were born not only of grief but guilt. Her parents had been on their way to see her that fateful day. Their visit was to be a surprise. Thanks to her job at that exclusive prep school, Caro had been kept busy the previous five months. In addition to being the counselor, she'd taken on an after-school tutoring job and had signed on as an assistant coach for the volleyball team.

"God, I'm so sorry." Bonnie scooted close enough on the couch so she could wrap an arm around Caro's shoulders.

"How horrible for you. I can't even imagine." Doreen, who sat on the opposite side, gave Caro's arm another squeeze.

The sympathy in the women's voices and the gestures of comfort were nearly Caro's undoing. Any minute now she was going to embarrass herself with a display of tears the likes of which she'd denied herself for five long years, fearing if she fell apart completely she might never put herself back together again. She couldn't afford to be broken now. For Cabot's sake, she had to remain whole.

"Thank you. You know, I'm feeling rather tired." Caro set her mug on the coffee table and rose to her feet. Her movements were far from graceful or fluid. "I hope you don't mind, but I think I'll turn in early."

The women, of course, weren't fooled. Nor had Caro expected them to be. Bonnie's overly bright smile brimmed with compassion, while Doreen nodded knowingly.

"You go right ahead. It's been a taxing day for you all around."

"We'll see you in the morning. I'll try to keep the kids from waking the entire household before dawn," Bonnie said. "But I can't make any promises since they're going to be eager to find their baskets."

Her words and the images they conjured up made Caro's heart ache worse. With a hastily issued "excuse me," she bolted from the room. She had just cleared the door when the lights flickered twice before going out. The inn went dark with the exception of the glow coming from the fire in the other room.

Caro heard the children squeal and then

settle down amid the soothing assurances of the adults.

"Isn't this an adventure?" she heard Bonnie claim.

A few of those forbidden tears leaked down her cheeks. It was the very thing she'd told Cabot when they'd left the Wendell estate five months ago, trading in a life of luxury and privilege for one far less pre-determined.

Caro couldn't bring herself to go back in, though that would have been the smart thing to do. Instead, she continued in the meager light to the staircase, rapping her elbow on the corner of the reception desk before coming to the stairs.

As she slid her feet carefully along the worn carpet of the treads, she thought she heard the creaking of a second set of footsteps. She stopped, blinked and widened her eyes in an attempt to see something, anything. But by this point everything was black as pitch.

"Hello?" she said at the same time as a foot came down atop hers. If not for the big hands that wrapped around her, the force of their bodies colliding might have sent her flying backward.

"Caro?" It was Jake.

"Yes. I was just on my way upstairs," she explained needlessly.

"The power's gone out." His words were equally unnecessary.

"The storm?"

"I wish I could say it was merely a blown fuse, but, yeah. The storm. We should go back downstairs."

"No!" She moderated her tone before continuing. "I was just on my way up to bed."

"Are you all right?" he asked. The hands gripping her arms tightened and she imagined him frowning again.

"Fine. Just tired."

"It's barely eight o'clock."

"Yes, but I've been up since dawn and it's been a rather eventful day," she replied, using the excuse his mother had given her.

"Eventful." He snorted. "You can say that again. I'll walk you up."

"Oh, there's really no need. I can find my way by myself," she told him with more confidence than she actually felt.

A light bounced off the wall at the head of the stairs before its beam turned on them and found them.

"I found a couple of flashlights and some

candles in the linen closet just down from my room," Dean said.

"Great. I'll take one. Caro's decided to turn in. I'll see that she doesn't run into any walls on her way to her room."

"So thoughtful," Dean said wryly. "Why do I get the feeling you wouldn't do the same for me?"

"Because I wouldn't. Hitting a wall or two would be good in your case," Jake replied. "The impact might knock some sense into you."

Dean laughed, apparently not offended by the insult. "Here you go." A second light winked on.

"Tell the others I'll be down in a minute."

"Okay." Dean's joking tone was gone when he asked, "Is that ancient furnace going to hold out?"

"If it goes, we have plenty of wood for the fire. We'll all be fine."

Caro found comfort in his words, delivered as they were with such authority. Jake had that air about him. He was a man who meant what he said. Everything would work out. Everything would be fine. The comfort lasted until they reached the bedroom. In her case, the raging snowstorm and loss of power were the least of her concerns.

"Hold this." He handed her the flashlight and rounded the bed.

The fire had burned down to embers that glowed red in the hearth. Jake added a couple more logs before stirring them with the poker and then blowing. It took mere seconds for the fire to catch and flicker back to life. Afterward, Jake rose to his feet.

"I feel guilty hogging a fireplace and one of the only working bathrooms in the place," she said as he came back around the bed.

"It's just for one night, Caro. Maybe two, depending on the roads and your car."

"Thank God!" He shot her a glance. "You know what I mean," she said. "The storm."

He let her off with a nod, but then his gaze sharpened. "You've been crying."

She reached up and brushed off the traces of her earlier tears. "Delayed reaction." She shrugged. "As I said, it's been an eventful day."

She thought that would be the end of it. Then he asked softly, "Are you in some kind of trouble?"

"Trouble?"

"You seem...desperate."

The word battered what remained of her defenses. Desperate. She was indeed. Yet she tried to deny it. Jake was a stranger, one who had made it clear he wasn't interested in taking on her problems. Even taking her in from the storm had seemed an imposition.

"I have a—"

"Deadline," he finished, sounding a little impatient. "I know."

"I have a son."

That news clearly caught him off guard.

"A son?"

"He's three and tomorrow is Easter."

The tears she'd done her damnedest to keep at bay broke free in a torrent. She dropped her head into her hands, too tired and heartsick to care about propriety or her own dignity. What did those things matter at a time like this?

Jake's first instinct was to ask the dozen questions that sprang to mind. That was the cop in him, always seeking answers and wanting things to add up. But the woman standing before him wasn't a case he was working. She was a stranger, the root of whose desperation he thought he now understood. So, he went with his second instinct. This one was rusty for lack of use.

He wrapped an arm awkwardly around her shaking shoulders and drew her closer.

She tensed at the contact. They both did. Though he suspected his reaction was more primal than hers. She felt good in his arms, right in a way he didn't care to analyze. Her hair was soft against his cheek. He forced himself to recall the reason he was holding her. This wasn't a lover's embrace. It was about offering comfort.

"It'll be okay. I think the snow is starting to slow down. The storm will be over by morning and then the county road crews will get busy. You'll be on your way before…you know it."

The fact was, it could be days before the roads were clear enough to travel.

"But not in time for Easter," she said miserably. The words were muffled against his shoulder and he felt another shudder pass through her.

"You said he's three. Kids that age, they're incredibly resilient. Celebrate Easter a couple days late with him. He won't care."

"Do you have children?"

He stiffened, pulled back, even as his mind was pulled into the past. He recalled one of the first entries he'd written in his journal:

Would you have been a boy or a girl?

A boy would be nice. I'd teach you how to do woodwork when you got older, like your grandpa taught me. This is assuming you had my temperament and not Dean's.

Then again, I have nothing against girls. I'd have been happy either way.

While the original idea of the diary had been so he could purge his anger and mourn his professional demise, he'd used it almost exclusively to express his pain, grief and, later, curiosity regarding the baby Miranda had aborted.

"No. No children."

Caro blinked, obviously waiting for more, given his earlier reassurance.

"But I...I spend a lot of time with Riley and Jillian." Or he had before moving to another state.

"They're nice kids."

"The best." But Jake's mind was on his child.

"Jake?"

He swallowed, forced himself to focus. "Where is your son right now?"

"In Burlington with his father and paternal

grandmother. It was his first extended visit with them since...well, in months. It was supposed to last a couple of days. It's been more than a week."

Ah. Custody battle with the ex, Jake concluded.

"You talked to him earlier on the phone," he said.

I love you.

Her words and soft expression took on a different meaning now. They hadn't been romantic in nature, but maternal. They were the words of a mother reassuring her child. Something inside him softened, ached. His child had never known that.

"Yes. He's scared, and he misses me."

"You said he was only supposed to be with his father for a couple days."

"That was our agreement. Cabot was to spend one weekend with his father and grandmother on Lake Champlain. They were going to celebrate Easter early since Cabot was supposed to be with me on the actual holiday."

"But the rules changed," Jake guessed.

Her eyes closed as she grimaced. "I should have known better. Truman has always been good at seeming reasonable in order to get

his way." Another sob shook her. "When he
didn't arrive at our meeting place at the designated time last Sunday evening, I called
him, and…was informed of a change in
plans."

"You'll be together soon, maybe even by
tomorrow night. Or the night after that at the
latest."

"You don't really believe that." She shook
her head sadly. "The roads might not be
passable for days and who knows when my
car will be ready. It's still sitting in a snowbank."

"It's going be okay, Caro. I promise. One
way or another, you'll be with your son,
even if that means I have to take you there
myself."

Jake didn't make promises easily. He was
the kind of man who needed to be sure he
could keep them before giving his word, because his word meant something. At least it
still meant something to him, even though
much of the public considered him a liar
who'd offer up any excuse as a way to cover
his butt.

"Why?"

"Your son…he deserves…he deserves…"
He couldn't finish. Because her son deserved

what Jake's child had been denied, a mother's unconditional love.

Even so, he couldn't be sure that was the only reason for his offer.

Caro stepped back and studied him. The fire's glow clearly showed the tracks of her tears. Jake's hands were more adept at holding guns and subduing suspects—or lately, wielding a hammer—than drying a woman's damp cheeks. But that's what he did. All the while, his gaze stayed on hers. Afterward, he flattened his palm against her cheek.

"You're a good man, Jake."

Her words were like balm to a wound that still festered. He studied her face in the flickering light. The sexual interest he felt didn't surprise him. That kind of chemistry was understandable and could be discounted easily enough, especially given his lengthy bout of celibacy. No, it was a different kind of need he was feeling, a yearning whose origin, whose very existence, he was at a loss to explain.

He lowered his head, wanting more than a kiss, which was foolish enough. It was because of what he wanted that he denied himself altogether, and in the end merely brushed his lips against her forehead.

Caro didn't seem insulted. She smiled at him. "You'll be a good dad someday."

She might as well have put a bullet in his heart. He stumbled back a step and swallowed convulsively.

"Jake?"

He didn't answer her. He couldn't. And so he left.

Long after Jake was gone, Caro stood where he'd left her, arms wrapped around her middle as she waited for her pulse to settle. She passed off her trembling as a result of the cold, though the room was plenty warm now with the fire that was crackling cheerily. The unexpected ache she felt deep inside was what really troubled her.

She wasn't entitled to feel it. He apparently felt the same, given the way he'd bolted from the room.

She tidied the bed linens, swallowing hard as she did so. She swore his scent wafted up from the sheets, curling about her much like the heat from the fire. It was a good thing she would be leaving as soon as the roads were cleared. She meant it when she'd told Jake he was a good man. Beneath the brooding and bruised exterior, he was just that. The sort of person who did what needed to be done. He didn't delegate the work to others. He rolled up his sleeves and did it himself.

But even good men could be trouble, especially when they came along at the wrong time. Just as bad men could seem good when a woman was blinded by grief.

Truman's words from their telephone conversation the week before haunted her.

"You belong with me, Caroline. You need me."

"I need no one," she'd protested.

"No, sweetheart. You're too delicate to be out on your own, especially raising our son."

"What do you mean by that?" she'd asked.

She'd thought she was beyond his manipulations. She'd thought she was well on her way to putting her life back together and creating a happy environment for her son.

It turned out she was wrong.

"I will not have our son raised by a grief-stricken single mother. Quite obviously, my dear, you are not thinking clearly. You need to come back by Easter and resume your life as my wife. No one here, other than Mother, of course, knows you tried to leave me."

"Where do they think Cabot and I have been?" she asked, incredulously.

"Staying at our condo in Belize. You didn't want to pass the long, cold winter here."

"And if I don't come back?" She'd had to swallow twice before asking the question.

"I will of course be forced to seek full custody of our son. You're not well, Caroline. Surely, you can see that. And I can't have our son raised by someone unstable."

"What...what are you talking about?"

"Mother agrees with me. She said it's a good bet you won't be allowed to visit Cabot without a social worker's supervision once a family court judge understands the full scope of things."

Ice had formed in her heart. The Wendells had that kind of pull and power, and she had none of their connections, much less their vast wealth.

Tonight, given the storm, he'd agreed to allow her one week's reprieve. But no more.

"I would hate to have to do this, Caroline. Surely, you must know that. But my lawyer is already preparing the paperwork and it will be filed if you don't return by the end of the week. Remember, I'm doing this for your own good as well as Cabot's."

"I'm doing all I can," she'd pleaded instead.

"Yes, and we'll see you soon. I know you'll do what's right," he'd finished.

What's right, she thought now with a sigh. Nothing in her life was going according to what was right, including these unexpected feelings that had welled up so suddenly for Jake McCabe.

Tightening the belt on her borrowed robe, Caro climbed into the bed. She pulled the covers up to her chin, doing her best to ignore thoughts of Jake occupying that very space, tangled up in those very sheets, only the night before.

Three hours later, the fire had burned down to mere embers again, Jake's scent lingered on her pillow like a promise and Caro was wide-awake.

CHAPTER FIVE

SURELY, CARO WOULD BE sound asleep by now, Jake reasoned as he crept quietly up the stairs.

He took care to bypass the treads that he knew squeaked the loudest. He just needed to slip into his room, grab a pair of sweatpants from the bureau and his toothbrush from the bathroom. Then he would be on his way back downstairs where his mother had already made up the lumpy couch with a sheet and a couple of old quilts.

The rest of the McCabe clan had turned in more than an hour ago after Bonnie and Dean had filled the kids' Easter baskets with goodies. Jake had watched his brother and sister-in-law scurry about the living room with a flashlight to find the best hiding spots, giggling like a couple of kids themselves as they did so.

He'd watched the bobbing lights and listened to their lighthearted banter. He'd never envied his brother anything—until now. A loving wife, children Dean adored and who adored him back. He was a lucky man.

Jake hadn't expected to ever have either of those things. Police work made relationships difficult. He'd watched the marriages of too many of the guys in his department crumble from the stress and uncertainty. He hadn't been willing to go through it himself. His decision had suited him just fine, too, until he'd met Miranda. She'd made him believe in happily-ever-after endings, even for a cop known for his sharp edges and hard shell. She'd made him believe he could have the kind of family he'd grown up in. The kind of family Dean had now.

Upstairs, Jake heard his father, the undisputed night owl of the bunch, snoring noisily as he passed the room in which his parents were staying. They were good people, deeply involved in their community, and considered pillars of it. They'd defended him doggedly and without reservation. It had nearly killed him to watch journalists put them through the media wringer. To see his mother exit a Women's Club of Greater Buffalo meeting only to be ambushed by a throng of reporters shouting questions and cameramen jostling for a position.

The final straw had come after his ex gave a tell-all exclusive to one of the local network affiliates detailing what she'd termed Jake's dark nature. Miranda had turned the times he'd come home after a hard shift and locked himself away in his woodworking shop into a nefarious ritual.

"I never felt like I truly knew him," she'd said at the end, dabbing her eyes.

Maybe she was right. He sure as hell didn't know the woman who'd sold him out. The woman he later learned was having an affair. The woman who'd decided she didn't want to bear their child, but just move on.

The following day, Bonnie was stopped outside Jillian's dance studio by the same television crew, looking for more dirt.

"Were you afraid of your uncle?" the reporter asked Jillian, who'd tried to hide behind her mother.

As Bonnie tried to push past the cameraman, the reporter said, "Did you ever see warning signs that the man wasn't up to his job and that innocent people would wind up dead as a result?"

"Mommy, what does the man mean? Why is he talking about Uncle Jake this way?"

The look of horror and confusion on Jillian's face would haunt him to his grave. It was then that he'd decided to leave town. He'd put his family through enough.

Jake reached his bedroom. To his relief, Caro had left the door ajar. He pushed it in slowly, gritting his teeth when the hinges creaked in protest. Just a little wider and he would be able to slip through the opening. When the door creaked a second time, however, he caught the silhouette of a woman jackknifing to a sitting position on the bed.

Time reeled backward and, for a moment, Jake relived the nightmare. A woman screamed; a baby cried. The echoes of gunfire long past rent the air. Silence followed, punctuated only by the broken pleading of the rookie cop under his command.

No! God, no! What have I done?

"J-Jake?"

Caro's voice snapped him back to the present. Although the room was dark, he didn't need to see her expression to know he'd probably scared her half to death. And no wonder, creeping in and then standing just inside the doorway near the foot of her bed breathing as heavily as some pervert.

"Sorry." He wiped a hand down his face and gathered up his wits. "Yeah. It's me. I just need... I just need...my toothbrush. Sorry," he muttered a second time as he stumbled in the direction of the bathroom.

Inside, he splashed cold water on his face. After blotting it dry, he leaned against the porcelain basin and exhaled slowly. He was grateful it was too dark to see his reflection in the mirror that hung over the sink. He probably looked as shaky as he felt.

Why wouldn't the past stay put?

He knew what a shrink would say. It was because nothing had been resolved, which was why the department psychologist had recommended further counseling when he'd agreed to resign. The way Jake saw it, no amount of counseling would change the facts. Besides, fixing up the old inn was keeping him busy. His mind and his hands equally occupied. It was therapy enough.

Or it had been.

Until just recently.

Caro was sitting on the side of the bed when he came out of the bathroom. She was clutching the lapels of the borrowed robe at her throat. She'd added a log to the fire, but it was slow to catch, spitting out only enough flame to allow him to read her expression. She didn't look frightened. She looked concerned. Not for herself, but for him.

"I'll stoke up the fire before I go," he offered. "You need to stir up the embers or that log you put on won't catch properly."

"The only fires I'm used to starting these days are the gas kind that go on with the click of a remote-control button," she admitted ruefully.

"Those are more practical." Jake knelt down and poked at the embers, coaxing out flames.

"I know, but I like the crackling sound a wood fire makes. It reminds me of being a kid and going on camping trips with my Daisy Scouts troop."

He angled to the side so he could peek at her over his shoulder. "You were a Daisy Scout? No offense, but I'm having a hard time picturing you pitching a tent and slathering up with bug repellent."

"Well, I did."

She notched up her chin. He found the defiant gesture way too sexy for his peace of mind.

"In fact, I was a tomboy till my early teens," she was saying. There was a smile in her voice when she added, "My dad used to tease me that I was the son he never had. As a joke, he'd call me Carl. It drove my mother crazy."

Jake definitely couldn't picture the ultra-feminine woman who was sitting on the edge of the bed being anything remotely boyish.

"Then what happened?"

"I discovered the opposite sex and decided I wanted to be a girl again."

"Good choice." When her brows rose, he cleared his throat and pushed to his feet. "I'll get out of your way now. I didn't mean to wake you. And, sorry if I scared you. I was trying to avoid both."

"You didn't wake me."

He noticed she said nothing about the scared part. Given the way she'd jackknifed off the mattress, he figured she didn't see the point in denying he'd given her a fright.

"Can't sleep?"

"No. I was exhausted earlier, but now?" Her laughter was bemused. Even so, he liked the sound of it. She was thinking about her son, no doubt.

Jake was thinking about him, too. He won-dered what her child was like; he wondered why the man who'd fathered him was no longer part of her life.

But all he said was, "If you're hungry there's more of my mom's chili in the fridge. You could heat some up. The stove is gas, so it still works even without the power."

"No offense, but if I have a bowl of Doreen's chili now, I doubt I'll sleep at all."

It was his turn to chuckle. "You can't say I didn't warn you about the heat."

"You did. But it was worth a little heartburn."

A smile bloomed on Caro's lips, drawing his attention to her mouth. The interest he kept trying to deny mocked him again. He swallowed and glanced away.

Picking up the thread of their conversation, he said, "She's won blue ribbons with it at the annual cook-off held in Niagara Square."

"My mother couldn't cook to save her life," Caro said. "My dad did all of that. He was quite good at it, although he came up with a few questionable combinations that even our golden retriever wouldn't touch."

This was the second time she'd mentioned her parents. The second time that, despite her smile, he'd detected a note of sadness.

"My mother told me earlier you'd lost them both in a car accident."

Caro's expression faltered as she nodded.

"Sorry."

"It's been five years."

"The amount of time doesn't matter. It still hurts." He cleared his throat. "I'd imagine."

"Yes. It does. Thank you."

"For what?"

"For understanding how much I still miss them. I try not to wallow in it or anything," she said.

"But you haven't forgotten them. And you never will."

She nodded. "They were on their way to see me when the accident happened."

Just as she'd been on her way to see her son when she'd slid off the road into the snowbank. The realization gave new insight into just how frightened she must have been. And just how desperate to risk life and limb in a storm to get to her child.

She stood then and gave the robe's belt a brisk yank. "You know, maybe a cup of tea would be nice. That is if you have any."

"Tea?" He shook his head. "Sorry, I'm not a big fan of the beverage."

"I'm shocked," she said, deadpan. "I had you pegged as a green-tea enthusiast."

He shook his head, grateful for the light topic and her teasing tone. He was more than happy to leave the discussion of tragedy behind, even though he'd been the one to initiate it.

"I like coffee. Strong and black."

"And, let me guess, thick enough to chew."

"Now you're catching on."

"I don't think I'm up for that."

"Me, either. Bonnie brought some hot cocoa to make for the kids," he said.

"And mini-marshmallows?"

"Is that how you take it?"

"Is there any other way?" she demanded on a laugh.

"How about with a little shot of peppermint schnapps thrown in?"

"Hmm. I've never had that. It sounds good. And a little more grown-up than the mini-marshmallows," she admitted.

"You can add those, too, if you want. It's not an either-or proposition."

"Thanks. I've had enough of those lately."

Curious, Jake nonetheless didn't ask what she meant.

* * *

They made their way downstairs with the aid
of the flashlight he'd left for her use earlier.
In the kitchen, in lieu of a kettle, Jake filled
a saucepan with water and switched on the
stove burner. As blue flames licked the bottom of the pan, he grabbed two heavy porcelain mugs from one of the cabinets and a
bottle of schnapps from another.

"Shine the light over here," he instructed.

Caro came over to stand next to him as he
rooted through a couple of grocery bags on
the counter. A moment later he had the hot-
cocoa mix. He handed her the bag of mini-
marshmallows.

"Don't worry. I'll share." At his confused
expression, she added, "You know you're
going to want some of these."

Half of his mouth rose in a smile that had
a curious effect on her insides. "Maybe just a
couple."

"Please. No one eats just a couple mini-
marshmallows," she said. "They're like potato chips. Half the bag is gone before you
know it."

He eyed her in the dim light. "You don't
look like the sort of woman to binge on junk
food."

"We all have our guilty pleasures."

The words hung in the air between them. Pleasures, guilty or otherwise, had been low on Jake's list of priorities these past several months. He hadn't forgotten what he liked, though. His gaze lowered to her mouth, settled on a pair of ripe lips that were slightly parted and ever so inviting.

"Don't forget yours," she said.

Gaze lingering on her mouth as his libido slipped toward fantasy mode, all he said was, "Hmm?"

"The schnapps."

"Schnapps?" He struggled through the haze of hormones.

"Peppermint schnapps to put in our hot chocolate. As guilty pleasures go, that outranks both marshmallows and potato chips."

He nodded. Perhaps, but other things had come to mind that trumped a shot of schnapps but good.

"It's definitely more adult," he agreed, only to regret his choice of words. Anything labeled *adult* added another layer of complexity to guilty pleasures.

He concentrated on the matter at hand, and began spooning cocoa mix into their mugs. Caro added a generous heaping of marshmallows to hers. He decided to pass. The water was boiling in the pan on the stove. He carefully poured it into the first cup. Caro stirred. They repeated the process. Then he added a shot of the peppermint schnapps to both. She stirred again.

"We make a good team," she noted.

Jake frowned. He was no longer part of any team. His loner status, his self-imposed exile, he'd embraced both these past several months. Why had they suddenly begun to chafe? His family, their surprise visit, the argument with his brother. The explanation fit perfectly. Until his gaze caught on Caro.

"Jake?" She smiled uncertainly. "Everything all right?"

Nothing had been right for a long time. Sometimes he was sure nothing would ever be all right again. He nodded anyway.

"Take these over to the table. I'll see if I can find some matches and we'll light the candle in the centerpiece my mom brought for Easter dinner."

"Oh, we shouldn't do that," Caro protested. "Save it for tomorrow."

"It's okay. My mom won't mind. She's never been one to put appearances over practicality."

He found some matches and started the wick. As soon as he was seated across from Caro, though, he wished he'd heeded her advice. The woman looked even lovelier in the intimate glow of candlelight. There were just enough shadows to add an aura of mystery.

Jake had always liked mysteries. He especially liked solving them. He had a few pieces of the puzzle. A son. A custody battle. Grief over her parents. But what was the rest of her story? He didn't doubt there was more.

Caro sipped from her mug, coming away with a foamy upper lip, which she licked clean. "Mmm. This is really good."

He sipped from his own mug to keep from groaning. In general, he wasn't much of a fan of hot chocolate, but add a splash of schnapps and a beautiful woman, and the stuff was ambrosia.

"I feel like we should have had a snowball fight or something first," she said.

"That can be arranged."

"No, thanks."

"Have you had many snowball fights?"

Her expression remained wistful. "Not

many, no. Only child, remember? It's kind of hard to have a snowball fight with yourself."

"What about friends, kids from the neighborhood? Didn't you ever have a battle with them?"

"A few times." She shrugged. "The boys usually started it."

"Boys are good at that," he agreed, thinking back to his own childhood and the times he'd lobbed a snowball at an unsuspecting pretty girl to get her attention.

"Mostly, after a big snow, I spent time with the neighborhood girls building snowmen. Not because I really wanted to."

He wagged a finger. "Tomboy, you said."

"That's right. Still, I always thought it would be fun to be included in one of the huge, all-out wars the boys were having."

Caro took another sip. This time she wasn't as successful at clearing the melted marshmallow residue as she'd been the first time. A bit of it clung to her upper lip. He licked his own.

"You get to live your childhood over now." Her brows drew together, so he clarified, "With your son. Having children and watching the delight they take in everything is like being a kid again."

"That's an interesting observation for a man without children."

"Dean…that's what he says. Of course, my brother never really grew up anyway."

She waved blotchy fingertips at him. "You get to do things like dye Easter eggs."

Since his own were the same unrecognizable shade, he couldn't help laughing.

"And play hide-and-seek," he added. He and the kids had engaged in a game shortly after the egg dying, mostly to keep the kids out of Bonnie's hair.

"I couldn't help noticing that you're very good at both, by the way."

Her lips bowed after she made that assessment, and his attention was drawn once again to that little patch of melted marshmallow on the top one. His mouth watered. He swallowed and glanced away.

"Thanks. One of the perks of being an uncle is you get to let your inner child out every now and then."

Earlier, Caro wouldn't have thought the brooding man had an inner child. He was full of surprises. She was full of questions. Curiosity trumped politeness, so she asked one.

"Do you plan to settle down someday and have a family of your own?"

Jake's demeanor changed then, as did his expression. Both turned rigid and guarded. His answer was flat and monosyllabic. "No."

It's not your business, she reminded herself. Even so, she heard herself prodding, "Never?"

His gaze remained focused on the fat, flickering candle that sat tucked amid greenery on the table between them. He was silent for so long, she didn't think he planned to answer her. It was probably just as well that he didn't. She was opening her mouth to apologize and change the subject when he spoke.

"I used to think I would." The words came slowly, as if pulled from some spot deep inside of him. Caro waited patiently for him to continue. "I'd met someone. We made it all legal. Then we settled in a fixer-upper we got for a steal in a neighborhood that our real-estate agent termed 'up and coming.'" Rough laughter followed. "That just meant the house needed a lot of work and the neighborhood was still really rough around the edges. But it was a lot of house for the money, and it had great potential."

Forget the house and neighborhood, Caro was still processing the wife part.

Jake McCabe had been married.

CHAPTER SIX

"Miranda."

He blinked in surprise, before glowering. "You know her?"

"No. No." Caro shook her head, even as she wanted to smack the side of it with her palm. With no graceful way out of the mess she'd created, she said vaguely, "I...I heard her name mentioned earlier and wondered who she was."

"You heard her name mentioned." He snorted. "I'm guessing you heard a lot more than that."

"No." The little white lie was warranted. No way was she going to tell him the context in which Dean had brought up the woman. "Sorry."

"I was, too." Bitter laughter followed. Jake's gaze never left the candle flame. Instead of being guarded, his expression now

JACKIE BRAUN   111

reflected betrayal and pain. "Sorry I met her.
I thought it was a lifetime deal. It turns out I
was wrong."

Having made a similar discovery herself,
Caro ached for him.

"What happened?"

He grunted, but he didn't tell her to go to
hell. She considered that a good sign. After
a moment, Jake said, "The short answer is
that when the going got tough, she got going,
keeping her baggage really light."

She cleared her throat. "And the long
answer?"

His gaze lifted to hers. In the glow of the
candle, his blue eyes narrowed not so much
in suspicion as in puzzlement.

"I don't like to talk about it."

"Oh. I understand. I'm sorry. I didn't mean
to pry."

He eyed her stoically for another long moment. She was getting ready to issue a second apology when he said, "Are you sure you
want to hear it?"

"Only if you're sure you want to tell me."

His head tilted to one side as he studied
her. "Why do I get the feeling that you're a
really good listener, Caro Franklin?"

"Because I am. You might say I'm a pro-fessional."

He didn't move, but she sensed he pulled back from her. "Head doctor?"

"School counselor."

Blue eyes blinked. "Yeah?"

"Why do I get the feeling you're sur-prised?" she asked, slightly insulted.

"I didn't expect...that."

"The career choice or the fact that I worked in the first place?"

"Both," he admitted.

"You have some preconceived notions where I'm concerned."

"Guilty."

"Why?"

"I don't know. I get the feeling there's more to you than meets the eye."

"That's because there is."

His eyes narrowed in assessment before he offered a curt nod. "Touché. So, where are you doing this counseling work?"

Her work at the private academy had paid handsomely and she'd enjoyed the work. The headmaster had assured her when she'd asked to extend her maternity leave another couple of months that he would hold her po-sition. Truman had other ideas.

"I'm sort of between full-time jobs at the moment, although I do work in a public school system outside Montpelier. Before I left him, my husband poisoned the well at my old place of employment."

"How'd he do that?"

"Perhaps *poisoned* isn't the right word. He made a very generous donation." So generous that the Wendell name would adorn the new science wing now under construction. "Let's just say that his family has the kind of money and connections that make people forget all about the promises they've made."

"Ah, dollar-sign amnesia."

She laughed, though there was nothing humorous about the situation.

I did it for your own good, Caro. You didn't need to work. You need to stay home with our son and let me take care of both of you.

The old sadness settled over her—Truman was never able to understand how stifling his brand of caring could be.

Jake said, "It's not the way you saw your life turning out, is it?"

Though he posed the question to Caro, she got the feeling it was also a statement that could be applied to his marriage.

"No," she admitted ruefully. "I was going for happily ever after."

It didn't surprise her when Jake snorted. His words, however, were unexpected. "I didn't believe in that sort of fairy tale myself until I met Miranda."

"If you don't mind my asking, what was she like?"

"Different from me, that's for sure. Different from anyone I'd ever met." He scrubbed a hand over his chin and shifted in his seat. "That was half the problem. We had very different interests, and our values…" A muscle ticked in his jaw, but Jake didn't elaborate.

"Opposites attract?" Caro offered.

"They shouldn't. It makes it harder to ride out the rough patches when you're always on different pages."

Caro nodded. She and Truman hadn't been in the same chapter most days.

Jake sipped his cocoa. "Miranda didn't like my job, which is sort of ironic considering it was how we met. I was a cop, and we were introduced at the city's annual Police Officers' Ball, which raises money for a local children's charity."

Jake was a police officer. That fit. He was

definitely the type of man who took charge
of a situation and then paid close attention to
the details. But it was something else he said
on which she homed in. His use of the past
tense.

"What made you give up police work?"

"You are a good listener." That muscle
worked in his jaw again. "Something...
happened under my command. A tragic
miscalculation that resulted in two civilian
casualties." He huffed out a breath and his
tone turned wry. "That's copspeak for two
innocent people wound up dead."

"God! That's horrible." Caro resisted the
urge to reach for Jake's hand. The rigid set of
his shoulders told her he wouldn't accept her
sympathy, as sincere as it was. "You blame
yourself," she guessed.

"It's impossible not to. I was the one in
charge. That means I'm responsible. It doesn't
matter that I wasn't the one who pulled the
trigger."

It wasn't as cut-and-dried as that, she was
willing to bet. But she said, "Is that when the
going got tough and your ex got going?"

He drummed the tabletop with his fingers. The sound echoed in the quiet kitchen.
"She said she couldn't take the shame and

ridicule." He angled his head to one side. "You see, I'm persona non grata back in Buffalo. The public was understandably shaken and outraged. One of those casualties I mentioned was a child...a little girl... even younger than your son."

His voice had turned hoarse with emotion and the fingers that a moment ago had drummed on the tabletop now bunched into fists.

"I'm so sorry."

His gaze connected with hers. Only the pain she saw there kept her from flinching when he replied harshly, "I don't deserve your sympathy or anyone else's. I'm here." One of his fists pounded the tabletop. Their cups rattled and the candle flickered. "Innocent lives were lost...." He lifted his shoulders in a helpless shrug as words failed him.

"Jake—"

He shook his head, cleared his throat. "Let me finish. Just so you understand how undeserved your sympathy is. An internal affairs investigation cleared me and the officer who fired the shots of any wrongdoing. But that poor rookie, he couldn't...he couldn't accept it. He put his service revolver in his mouth one month after the findings."

Jake's hands were no longer balled into fists. He sat in the candlelight studying them now, and Caro wondered, did he see blood there? He shouldn't. Even told from his obviously biased view, she couldn't see where he deserved all of the blame. Accidents happened. Even the best-laid plans went awry. Perfection, as Caro knew from painful experience, was impossible to achieve.

"You said an investigation cleared you and the officer of wrongdoing. Have you ever cleared yourself?" she asked softly.

Jake ignored her question and continued. "The public furor didn't die down after the investigation. There had been a couple other incidents before that in which the public felt police used unnecessary force. A wrongful-death lawsuit was filed by the victims' family. There were demonstrations downtown. I was burned in effigy."

"That must have been horrible."

"For my family," he agreed. But she didn't buy that it hadn't affected Jake, as well.

"Some big-shot activists came to town then and basically called for my head on a silver platter. By then, Miranda and I were already estranged. She was staying with a friend, supposedly working through her feelings." His bitter laughter echoed in the quiet room. "It turned out her friend was also her lover, and she…and she…well, she was already in the process of moving on."

"Sorry." How many times could she say that, Caro wondered. Yet no other word applied.

It didn't surprise her when he deflected her sympathy once again. "It was hell on my folks, though they never complained. But the way the media went after them…" He shook his head.

Which, Caro thought, explained what someone like Jake was doing in rural Vermont, acting as a handyman and fixing up an inn that had seen much better days.

"So you quit your job and came to the Green Mountains," she said.

"In a roundabout way. I was asked to leave the department. My union rep wanted to fight it, but it seemed like a no-brainer to me. The city was in an uproar. It was promising to be a long, hot summer as it was. Things were only going to get worse if I stayed."

"It doesn't seem right."

"It was for the best."

"For whom?"

He ignored the question. "It was all handled very quietly. My family no longer had media stalking them. And Miranda... Miranda had..." Jake shook his head and said with a finality born of pain, "Our marriage was over."

"Sorry." The word was inadequate, she knew, but heartfelt. "It hurts to find out you were wrong about the person you planned to spend the rest of your life with."

His gaze connected with hers over the candle flame. "Would that be the voice of experience talking?"

Caro nodded uncomfortably. Just that quickly, he'd exchanged places with her in the hot seat.

"How long were you married?"

"A little more than four years."

She didn't stop to consider that her words could be misleading. Her marriage *was* over. Nothing would change that. No matter what she was forced to do to remain near her son, she wouldn't be Truman's wife in any meaningful sense of the word.

"Did he...cheat?"

"On me?" She blinked, shook her head. "Truman's too tied to his mother to ever think about cheating on her with two women. Marriage to me was enough of a stretch for him."

"Never cut the apron strings?"

"Wh-what?" She felt her face heat, realized what she'd said. Now was usually the time she went into full retreat mode. Deny and retract. Instead she sighed. "Exactly. And Susan made it clear from the beginning she didn't think I was good enough for her son."

"What did your husband have to say about that?"

"Truman felt I needed improvement in certain areas to fit in better with his social circle. I'm a diamond in the rough, you see. And he spent four years trying to file off all those odd angles and edges."

Jake frowned. "Oh, I don't know about that. From where I'm sitting, you look pretty perfect."

Callused fingers found hers on the table and gave a brief squeeze. It might as well have been a full-fledged caress the way her body reacted. She swallowed, not sure what to say, nor what to make of the heat that streaked through her system.

"You don't believe his assessment?" Jake

pressed, mistaking her silence for self-doubt.

"No. I don't think I ever really did, but I was not quite myself when we met and he had a way of making it seem as if he was only looking out for my best interests."

"Manipulative."

She sighed. "Yes, but he does have some good qualities. For instance, I know that he truly loves our son. He would never hurt him."

"That is an important quality." Jake sounded oddly wistful.

Indeed it was, Caro thought. But it wasn't enough to base a marriage on. She decided to change the subject. "Getting back to you, do you miss police work?"

"Yes and no. I liked helping people and having a hand in cleaning up the streets. But some days…" His expression turned dark.

She imagined he'd seen things no person should ever see. Her counselor skills kicked in and she prodded, "Some days what?"

"It's not an easy life. When you're on the job, you have to be hyperaware. You can't let your guard down. Ever. Then you go home and…"

"It's hard to turn it off."

His gaze connected with hers. "Exactly. A lot of guys knock back a few cold ones to unwind. Some end up knocking back a few too many a little too often."

"They become alcoholics."

He nodded.

"What did you do to unwind?" she asked softly. No way she believed he'd succumbed to addiction. He was too in control for that.

"I built things. When I was a kid, my dad was always working on some project or another. He had a workshop in the basement."

"My dad had a basement workshop, too," Caro said. On a chuckle, she added, "He didn't really make anything. I think he just went down there in the evenings to spend time in an estrogen-free zone."

"A man cave, huh?" Half Jake's mouth rose. He had a sexy mouth, wide and mobile.

"I guess so." She managed to sound normal, even as she felt oddly breathless.

"My dad's specialty was woodworking. He made some first-rate cabinetry, good enough that he could have sold it, but he mostly gave it away to friends and family. He considered it a hobby, something he did after a long day at the office. He was in insurance for more than thirty years. He's semiretired now."

"What about your mom?"

"Full-time homemaker, for the most part. She had odd jobs here and there, but she made a point to be home when Dean and I were home, so that made a full-time career tough." His tone turned wry. "When we were kids, Dean and I considered ourselves deprived because it was only on the rare occasion that we ate fast food, where most of our friends were hitting drive-throughs on a regular basis."

"Same here. I don't think I truly appreciated all of the sacrifices my parents made until I became a parent myself. You'll do anything for your child. Anything."

"When you're given the chance."

It was an odd thing to say, especially given his tone. "What do you mean?"

He shook his head. His expression wasn't so much dark now as it was pained. He cleared his throat. "Anyway, my dad was a willing teacher as long as you were a willing student. Woodworking takes time. Dean never had the patience to see a project through."

"But you did."

"I did," he agreed on a nod.

It hadn't taken Caro long to determine

that while Jake and Dean shared many of the same physical characteristics, they were very different in personality. Dean was spontaneous and outgoing, where Jake proceeded with care and caution. Yet right now, in the wee hours of the night, he was sitting in the kitchen with a virtual stranger, and they were sharing schnapps-laced cocoa and secrets.

Perhaps the brothers weren't so different after all. Perhaps Jake was not nearly as rigid and standoffish as he first appeared. He'd certainly surprised her with his candor in discussing his life. And she'd surprised herself with what she'd admitted to him about hers.

This wasn't like her, either. Caro tended to be a private person. She hadn't admitted the details of her fractured relationship with Truman to some of her closest friends. So why Jake? She tucked away the question to explore another time. Eager to fill in another piece of his puzzle, she asked, "What did you build to relieve stress after a hard day of police work?"

"Chairs. Rockers, to be specific. The old-fashioned sort you often see on the front porches of older homes."

"Oh, I love those! Not that I have any. Or

that I have a front porch." Her smile dimmed a little. "I'm living in an apartment." It dimmed a little more. "For now. What are your plans for this place?"

"I'm not sure," he admitted.

"Do you want to run it?"

"No." Jake's reply was quick and automatic, the very answer he'd given his family just the day before. But then he frowned. Running the inn had never been part of the plan. Not that he'd actually had a plan when he'd signed the papers and bought the place. He'd just been looking for something to do and a place to do it. And the department's payout made a lot of things possible. But now? "I don't know."

"I can see you here."

He blinked, clearly surprised. "Yeah? As an innkeeper?"

She shrugged and smiled. "Maybe as the owner-slash-handyman. You should probably leave the front desk to someone else."

"Thanks." But Jake laughed. He wasn't exactly the warm-and-welcoming sort these days and he knew it. Still, it was interesting that Caro didn't think he was wasting his time here. For that matter, neither did his family, even though they questioned his reasons for buying the inn.

"This place was something back in its day. My dad stumbled across it on a business trip once. He brought our family here at different times over the years. We were here for the fall colors in the fall, for skiing in winter and hiking and berry-picking in summer. And in the spring, Dean and I once traipsed after the workers as they tapped the maples for sap. The inn used to sell the syrup."

"Restoring it must give you a sense of satisfaction, then. And purpose. Especially after everything that happened in Buffalo."

He made a noncommittal sound, not at all sure he liked how quickly she'd reached that conclusion. Not at all sure he liked how well she understood him.

Their hot cocoa was long gone and the candle had burned down considerably, its sides caving in on the hollowed-out center. So much for his mother's Easter dinner centerpiece, Jake thought. But with no real regret. He'd enjoyed sitting in the semidark of the quiet kitchen with Caro.

Talking.

Even if every now and then when she tilted

her head a certain way and her gaze caught the reflection of the candle, he'd also found himself wanting to do a lot more.

It surprised him that he'd told her everything that he had, even if he'd left out a lot of the uglier details and how he felt about them.

After he'd bared his soul, he'd half expected her to shy away from him. Politely, of course. She was a guest under his roof, after all. But he'd sensed no revulsion, no attempt to establish distance. She'd listened and, oddly enough, that had made him want to open up.

Talking to Caro wasn't like talking to the department psychologist, who was a nice enough guy with a batch of diplomas on his office wall to attest to his education and expertise. Nor was it like talking to his family, who were as angry at him for not fighting to salvage his reputation as they were with city officials for tossing him to the wolves.

No, talking with Caro was different, though he wasn't sure exactly how. Or why, even now, he wanted to keep doing it, and maybe probe into her past a little.

Instead, he pointed to the candle and said, "I guess we should call it a night."

"Yes. It's late."

Neither of them moved, though. The candle flickered invitingly as the silence stretched. Caro was the one who finally stood. While she carried their mugs to the sink and rinsed them, Jake collected the flashlight. When she finished, he flipped it on and blew out the flame.

She pulled the robe's belt tight, secured the lapels at her throat. "Well, good night."

"I'll walk you up. The fire will need another log or two."

"Oh. Okay."

The steps groaned and creaked under their feet. Jake half expected his mother to materialize at the top of the stairs, like she used to when he was a kid creeping in past curfew. But the door to the room in which his parents were staying remained closed.

When they reached the bedroom, his plan was to stoke the fire to life and make his exit before things could get more awkward. As it was, he felt as if he were walking a date home after a night out, his palms sweating as he anticipated things he had no right to anticipate.

As he'd suspected, the fire was down to embers again. In the morning, he would have to restock the wood bin to the side of the hearth. Only a couple of logs remained. They would be enough to see Caro comfortably through what remained of the night. It took only a couple of minutes to accomplish his goal while Caro stood patiently behind him, shining the flashlight until its beam was no longer necessary.

Jake rose to his feet and dusted his palms together. "That should keep you warm enough until the morning."

"Thanks."

She handed him the flashlight, which he tapped against his thigh. Words bubbled up inside him. Caro had that effect on him, apparently. "Thank *you*."

Her eyelids flickered in surprise. "For what?"

"I'm not sure." His laughter was strained and self-conscious. "For listening, I guess."

She smiled. "I told you I was good at it."

"Yes, you did." He reached for her hand and gave it a gentle squeeze. Her fingers were fine-boned and slender, and her skin was soft, in direct contrast to the calluses that thickened his palms. "And you are. A very good listener, even for someone like me who doesn't much like talking...about stuff."

"Sometimes it's easier to converse with a stranger than it is with family members or close friends," she offered.

He nodded, but he couldn't help thinking that her theory was flawed. Caro didn't seem much like a stranger to him, even though in the strictest sense of the word that was exactly what she was. They'd known one another less than twenty-four hours. That their paths had crossed at all was as much a fluke as the late-season storm.

"I guess so."

He was still holding her hand he realized. The bigger surprise was that he was in no hurry to release it and leave. He glanced away and his gaze caught on the bed. The covers were every bit as rumpled as he usually left them. He swallowed, because messing them up was what he had in mind now, but not out of restlessness. When he looked back at Caro, she seemed to understand the prurient direction of his thoughts. Her lips had parted and her breathing had turned labored.

"I really should go. Right now," he whispered, more for his own benefit than hers.

The words held an odd note of desperation. Even so, he failed to heed them. Instead of releasing her hand and heading for the door, he pulled her toward him.

Jake did it slowly, giving her time to push away. She didn't, and so he lowered his head, moving slowly again. That anticipation he'd tried to ignore built right along with need. Finally, his mouth found hers. When her lips parted in acceptance, it was all he could do to hold back his moan of pleasure.

Caro fit him perfectly. Not only her mouth but her body, which was molded to his from chest to thigh. She was thin, but with curves in all the right places. He knew this for a fact now, because his hands sought them out as desperation and need broke free of their restraints.

"Jake."

She sighed his name as his mouth cruised down her neck. She smelled of his soap and hot cocoa, a combination as unexpectedly beguiling as the woman herself. When he would have stopped, she cupped his face and brought his mouth back to hers for a second taste of heaven. All the while, the bed just behind them beckoned, taunting him and testing his resolve.

Good sense finally prevailed, battling to the surface through a turbulent sea of hormones. Sex with Caro would be a bad idea. As soon as the roads were passable and her car was fixed, she would be on her way. He didn't know if he would ever see her again. He wasn't even sure he wanted to. He wasn't in the market or in the mood for a relationship, and she didn't strike him as the type to go for no-strings sex.

For that matter, he wasn't big on bed-hopping himself. Perhaps if he were, he wouldn't have spent the past several months sexually frustrated.

She deserved better than what little he had to offer her. She deserved someone who was emotionally whole. Someone whose reputation wasn't besmirched. It took a Herculean effort, but Jake found the strength to break away.

"I don't think this is a good idea," he said inanely when he finally caught his breath.

She blinked. Even in the low light he saw her cheeks turn pink. And no wonder. He'd been the one to initiate the kiss. She'd done nothing wrong. Even so, she was the one to apologize.

"I'm sorry. I shouldn't have—"

"Caro, don't." He took her by the shoulders, hoping to give his words more sway. "It was my fault. Mine."

"I kissed you back," she surprised him by replying.

Did she have to say something like that? For that matter, did she have to look so damned lovely and confused in the flickering light of the fire?

"It was my fault," he said again.

"I don't believe you forced me." Her tone was crisp now. God help him, but he liked it, almost as much as he liked seeing the determined arch of her brows. The last thing he wanted was for her to cry. Not only because then he would feel like an even bigger heel than he already did, but because he liked seeing her spunk. Something told him she didn't exercise it as often as she should.

She pushed her hair back from her face. A moment ago his fingers had been caught up in that silken mass. They were itching to be there again. He released her shoulders and fisted his hands at his sides to keep from doing something foolish.

"I didn't force you, but—"

"You're right," she interrupted. "This isn't a good idea."

"We barely know one another," he agreed, though that was the least of it to his way of thinking.

She shook her head, swallowed and leveled him with her reply. "Legally, I'm still married, Jake."

CHAPTER SEVEN

CARO STOOD AT THE BEDROOM window early the next morning, and gazed out at the landscape. The inn was in a clearing tucked amid a stand of trees, but rising up beyond them was the distinctive, rocky summit of Camel's Hump. This day it was covered in white, as was everything as far as Caro's eyes could see.

Just after dawn, she'd awoken to the sound of children's voices and the scampering of small feet. Jillian and Riley were up and running around. She heard the squeak of stair treads and knew they were heading down. They were shooed back up in a moment by their grandmother. Caro had hugged a pillow to her chest as she'd lain in Jake's big bed listening to their squeals of excitement and their parents' numerous attempts to shush them. The kids even whispered loud, which made her smile and want to cry at the same time. Cabot whispered loud, too.

This was what she should be doing. She'd wanted to call her son right then. She didn't care if she woke up the entire Wendell household in the process, the need was so great. But along with the electrical power, the storm had knocked out the inn's telephone line. With her cell still not getting a signal, she had no way to reach Cabot. She had no way to reassure him that she would be with him as soon as was humanly possible.

Mommy, I miss you.

He'd told her that the day before during their all-too-brief phone conversation. Those four words, uttered in his high pitch, had torn at her heart. Cabot was her focus. He was her life. Which was why long after Riley and Jillian found their Easter baskets, Caro remained in her room upstairs, contemplating the events of the previous night and wondering how they'd happened.

Jake had kissed her. But what appalled her was not that she had allowed it, but that she'd kissed him back. And with enough passion that they both had been left shaken and aroused.

She'd forgotten what that kind of desire

felt like. Or, maybe, she admitted now, she'd never experienced its like before. Perhaps that was why, even when it hadn't been wise, she had leaned toward him again and initiated a second kiss, luxuriated in the texture of his mouth and the feel of his hard body pressed against hers.

She wasn't free to kiss a man like that, regardless of the state of her marriage and how she felt about Truman. And she certainly wasn't free to want to do more.

She pinched her eyes closed now, but it didn't matter. She could still see Jake's face when she'd told him she was married.

His anger, she'd expected. Disbelief, too, given what had just transpired. But she was unprepared for the odd mix of disappointment and betrayal that had passed over his face before his features hardened into an indecipherable mask.

"You're not divorced," he'd said slowly.

"No. Truman and I are still legally married."

"You're separated then."

"We have been. For several months my son and I have been living in an apartment in Montpelier."

The rigid set of Jake's shoulders had

relaxed fractionally at the news. "So, you're in the process of getting divorced."

"I was."

He shook his head. "What kind of answer is that? Are you getting a divorce?"

"No." It was a difficult word to say aloud, nearly as difficult as it was for her to accept. "Jake, I—"

It was all she managed to get out before he'd held up a hand and stopped her. "Don't. There's really nothing more to say, Caro."

With that, he'd gone.

Now, she wasn't sure how she was going to face him. As it was, she was having a hard time facing herself. But she couldn't stay in her room all day.

"Enough with the self-pity," she murmured, giving the belt of the borrowed robe a yank.

It was time to see about her clothes, the roads and her car.

Over the rim of his coffee cup, Jake watched Caro enter the living room. Her hair was pulled back in a simple ponytail and her face free of makeup. She was dressed in the wool trousers and cashmere sweater she'd had on the day before. They were a little worse for

wear, especially the pants. The snow hadn't
been kind to her dry-clean-only goods. It
didn't matter. She looked beautiful. And out
of his league, especially now that he knew
she was married.

He sipped his coffee, grimaced. It wasn't
the strong brew that left such a bitter taste
in his mouth. She hadn't seemed the sort of
woman who would lie or cheat. Of course,
Miranda had had him fooled, too.

The children, still clad in their pajamas,
ran to where she stood in the doorway.
Fueled by sugar and excitement, they talked
and all but tripped over one another as they
showed her the bounty the Easter Bunny had
left for them.

"Want some of my jelly beans?" Jillian
asked. "The pink ones are my favorite. I
don't like the black ones."

"The black ones are yucky," Riley agreed.
"You can have all of mine if you want."

"I thought you were saving those for me,"
Jake said.

Caro's gaze connected with his briefly before she glanced away. Her cheeks flushed
as she moistened her lips before opening her
mouth to speak. Whatever she'd been about
to say, she changed her mind.

"I'll save you mine, Uncle Jake," Jillian offered. "Riley can give his to Caro. That will make it fair."

Children and fairness. It was a code they lived by. But it was a flawed code. Soon enough they would learn that life wasn't fair. Such a guarantee wasn't even possible. If life were fair, Caro would be with her son and husband right now, rather than disturbing Jake's peace, and Jake would have a child of his own.

Bonnie called the kids from another room, and they scampered out. Caro remained in the doorway, even though she looked uncomfortable and eager to leave. Perversely, he wanted her to stay.

"Good morning," she managed at last.

"Did you sleep well?" He threw it out as a challenge. He certainly hadn't. Between the lumpy sofa and his switched-on libido, he'd barely managed to close his eyes before the kids had roused him searching for their baskets.

"Yes. Thanks."

Liar. The dark smudges under her eyes told him otherwise. But he didn't call her on it.

She motioned toward the window with a hand whose third finger should have been adorned with a wedding band. "The snow stopped."

"Sometime around four." He knew, because he'd been awake.

"It's a new day, full of sunshine and promise." Yet her smile was uncertain.

"That's appropriate since it's Easter."

Hope, rebirth, salvation. That's what the holiday was about. He hadn't felt any of those things in a very long time. Nor had he cared. He'd felt dead inside. Defeated.

For reasons he couldn't quite grasp, that seemed to be changing.

"Jake, I want to apologize again," Caro said. "I wish…I wish things were different."

He'd spent too much time on futile wishes. He pushed to his feet and crossed to where she stood. "Look, let's just forget about it, okay?"

Her expression remained perplexed, but she nodded slowly.

"No harm, no foul, Caro. It was just a kiss."

As he started for the stairs, Jake wondered if she believed that any more than he did.

His room was tidy. She'd made the bed, folded the clothes he'd left lying over the chairs. Even though nothing in it belonged to

Caro, he swore it bore her stamp. He pulled on fresh jeans and a sweater, shaved and brushed his teeth. Though he didn't plan to, he settled on the edge of the bed and pulled his journal from the nightstand.

It had been nearly a month since he'd written anything in it. He flipped to the page where he'd left off and found a pen.

Today is Easter. Your grandparents, aunt, uncle and cousins are here with me at the inn. Their visit was unexpected. Your cousins are running around downstairs right now, hopped up on sugar and having a ball. You'd be too small to keep up with them. But next year...

The inn also has its first guest. Her name is Caro Franklin. She has a three-year-old son. She's so eager to see him she was driving through a nor'easter when her car went off the road.

His pen stilled and he gazed out the window. She also had a husband she wasn't so eager to see, but to whom she was returning anyway. She was married and had been separated, but she said there wasn't going to be a divorce. She'd said he was manipulative.

And Jake's first impression of Caro was that she was desperate. He tapped the pen against the page. Something wasn't adding up.

Doreen and Bonnie were in the kitchen peeling potatoes when Caro entered. Given the mound of skins in the sink, preparations for the afternoon's feast were well under way. But that wasn't why she felt guilty and oddly self-conscious.

"Good morning," the women said in unison.

"Good morning."

They hadn't a clue what had gone on the previous evening, but that didn't stop Caro from feeling as if the words *I kissed Jake* were tattooed on her forehead.

"Are you hungry?" Doreen asked.

"A little."

The older woman set her peeling knife aside. As she wiped her hands on a dish towel, she said, "What would you like for breakfast? We have eggs, bacon, bread for toast and a little leftover coffee cake if you'd prefer something sweet."

"The coffee cake sounds good."

Caro figured she could manage that herself, but before she could cross to the counter,

Doreen was already pulling back the plastic wrap and reaching for a knife.

"Oh, I can do that," Caro said. "You don't need to wait on me."

"Nonsense. Go and sit." Doreen motioned toward the table with the business end of the blade. "You're company. I won't hear of it."

"Better do as she says," Bonnie said on a laugh.

"Yes. It only took this one a few years to take her own advice," Doreen teased. "And by then she was family and I put family to work."

The women shared a chuckle. Caro envied their obviously close relationship. It was more like that of a mother and daughter or even of two friends, whereas all of her dealings with her mother-in-law were strained if not outright unpleasant. It was rare that Caro and Susan shared a laugh, unless it was over something cute that Cabot did. Even then it wasn't long before Susan found something to criticize.

Isn't it time he had a haircut?

His cheeks look flushed. Are you sure you put on sunscreen before setting off to the beach?

You really need to have a firmer hand with him when it comes to sweets.

Susan had probably already confiscated his Easter basket, assuming it had any edible treats in it.

From somewhere in the inn came a couple of high-pitched shrieks and the sound of racing feet.

"How much candy do you figure Dean's let them have since I told them no more?" Bonnie asked. "I'd better intervene. At this rate, there won't be anything left in their baskets by nightfall."

As Bonnie left the kitchen, Jake entered. He was dressed in jeans and a wool crewneck, over which he'd already pulled his shearling coat. His gaze lingered on Caro a moment until his mother said, "Where are you off to?"

"I thought I'd chop some more wood."

"There looks to be plenty outside the back door."

He shrugged. "It goes quick."

Caro watched his fingers make fast work of the buttons on the shearling coat. And though she tried not to, she recalled how those hands had felt caressing her through the robe.

The door swung closed and his heavy footsteps echoed down the hall to the back entrance.

Doreen frowned. "I wonder what's happened?"

A bite of coffee cake nearly caught in Caro's throat. "Wh-what do you mean?"

"There's enough cut wood to see this place through till next spring." The older woman shook her head. "No, something's on his mind. Something more than…"

She left the thought unfinished and resumed peeling potatoes. Caro stood and carried her dishes to the sink.

"Are you sure I can't help out with the meal preparations?" she asked, despite knowing the answer.

"Positive. Go." Doreen made a shooing motion. Even though the older woman smiled, Caro recognized a mother's worry in the line that had formed between her brows.

Movement caught her eye as she passed the big picture window that looked out from a small sitting room on the side of the inn.

Jake stood amid huge piles of split wood. What appeared to be an entire forest's worth of logs were stacked behind him. Dean was outside, too. Unlike his older brother, he held a mug of coffee instead of an ax, and the expression on his face was amused rather than fierce. As she watched, Jake placed a log on the flat surface of the tree stump that served as a chopping block. Feet planted shoulders' width apart, he raised the ax high over his head, bringing it down with such force that Caro knew his mother was right. Something was on his mind. Despite his "no harm, no foul" speech, she had a good idea what it was.

Through the window, she heard the crack of steel meeting wood. The log shuddered and split in two. Jake rested only a moment before selecting another piece and repeating the process. Dean, meanwhile, was sipping coffee and laughing. Caro frowned as guilt nipped her again.

She should have been more forthcoming. She should have told him that legally she was still Caroline Franklin Wendell and would remain such.

Till death do us part.

Now it seemed more like a life sentence than a treasured promise. Still, for Cabot's sake, she would honor her vows as best she could, especially the one about forsaking all others.

Until yesterday, the two she'd figured would give her the most problems were to love and to cherish. But she hadn't expected to meet Jake or to become so hopelessly attracted to him in so short a time. And she certainly hadn't imagined that anything romantic would transpire between the pair of them, even as it became clear that the growing attraction she felt was mutual.

As if Jake knew Caro was watching him, his gaze lifted from the log to her. Awareness shot through her like an electrical current as the moment stretched. She lifted one hand in what passed for a wave. Instead of lowering it afterward, however, she rested it against the cool glass. She might as well have been reaching for the unattainable. That's what he was.

"Hmm. What have we here?" Bonnie joined Caro at the window.

Caro jerked her hand away. "Nothing!" At the other woman's confused expression, she offered a nonchalant shrug. "They're just chopping wood."

Bonnie let out a snort of laughter. "*They*

aren't chopping wood. Jake is. And, as usual, Dean is standing around watching."

She undid the latch and opened the window just wide enough to holler out, "Hey, hot stuff. Let's see what you've got. Jake's putting you to shame."

Dean set his coffee mug aside and took the ax from Jake, making a show of flexing his muscles first for his wife's benefit. Bonnie giggled like a schoolgirl, even as she rolled her eyes.

"He's not nearly as buff as Jake. But I'll keep him."

Caro swallowed. Not nearly as buff indeed.

In no time at all a full-fledged competition was under way. The men had stripped off their heavy coats and Jake had shucked his sweater. They stood in their shirtsleeves, puffs of white breath offering proof of their exertion. Despite the freezing temperatures, their foreheads were dappled with sweat that glistened in the bright sun. Caro watched in fascination. Who knew men could look so sexy chopping wood? One man in particular.

"Would you look at those fools," Bonnie said. "By the time they're done, there won't be a tree standing in all of the Green Mountains."

Caro murmured in agreement even as she continued to admire Jake's form with the ax.

Bonnie offered an appreciative hum. "Still, I've got to admit it's kind of a turn-on to watch."

It was definitely that. But this time, Caro didn't make a sound. She merely stood at the window with her bottom lip caught between her teeth, damned by attraction and useless wishes.

Bonnie rapped her knuckles on the glass, gaining both men's attention before opening the window a second time.

"In the name of saving the trees, I declare a tie between you two great big ol' he-men."

Dean grinned wolfishly. "So, what's my prize?"

"I'll show you later," Bonnie teased with a throaty chuckle and a bob of her eyebrows.

Jake's gaze was on Caro. Even as he swiped his forearm over his brow, he never looked away.

"What's my prize?" he asked.

She had nothing to give him, nothing that

she was free to give, but that didn't stop her heart from thumping foolishly.

From the corner of her eye, she caught Bonnie's speculative look. She had little doubt Dean sported a similar expression. Luckily, the children, who were bundled up in their snowsuits, bounded into view then, and all attention turned to them.

Outside, Jake scooped the little boy up into his arms, much as he had the day before in the living room. Riley squealed with delight. Caro pictured Jake doing the same with Cabot. The image was so vivid and perfect it brought tears to her eyes. Truman wasn't much for horseplay. Bedtime stories were more his thing. Like his mother, he preferred peace and quiet. Whereas Caro delighted in Cabot's infectious laughter and unbridled enthusiasm.

Blinking the moisture from her eyes, she murmured, "Jake's really good with kids."

"The best. He would have made a great dad."

"Would have?"

Bonnie cleared her throat. "I mean, he *will* be a great dad. You know, someday."

The woman's flushed cheeks and guilty expression, however, told Caro that wasn't what she'd meant at all.

CHAPTER EIGHT

WHAT'S MY PRIZE?

He'd been foolish to ask the question, and even more foolish to be disappointed when Caro hadn't answered it, Jake thought as he stacked the newly split wood.

As usual, Dean was off playing with the kids, leaving him to do the work. He didn't mind. He needed something to do to take his mind off Caro. Not that he was succeeding.

Especially when he turned to find her striding through the snow in his direction. Now his labored breathing wasn't all the result of physical exertion. She had on her fashionable waffle-print down parka, but she'd borrowed a hat and mittens, and had found more sensible footwear. Unless he missed his guess, those were his mother's boots swallowing up her feet.

"I was thinking about going back to my

car. I'd love fresh clothes and to see if the main road has been cleared and a mechanic has been by."

"Are you planning to walk?"

Her chin lifted. "If need be."

He smiled, perversely pleased with her reply. "I have a better idea."

Until this past winter, the inn's old sleigh hadn't been out of the barn in who knew how many years. Half a dozen at least, Jake had figured, gauging from the rust on the runners when he'd come across it in the fall. It was a good thing he'd fixed it up, including a haphazard patch job on the seat cushions, which had mainly been to keep the mice from making more nests. He decided not to mention that to Caro as he hitched up Bess.

The harness bells jangled merrily.

"I heard those through the storm yesterday. And then you were there, a man on horseback riding to my rescue." She smiled at him.

"You thought I was an angel," he reminded her.

"I thought I was dead."

Gruff laughter escaped. "Well, that explains it."

"Explains what?"

"Why you thought I was heaven-sent. As I think you've figured out, I'm no angel." Especially given the direction his thoughts kept trying to head.

"But you are a hero." Even as he shook his head to deny her words, she said, "You saved me, Jake."

"Right time, right place."

"Adds up to the same thing." But she lightened her tone. "Who knew I'd owe my survival to a pair of feuding brothers?"

"I guess Dean is useful for something after all."

Riley and Jillian rounded the corner of the inn. Apparently they'd heard the bells, too.

"Uncle Jake! Uncle Jake! Can we go, too?" Jillian asked.

His gaze settled on Caro, and though he knew he was playing with fire, he said, "Not this time."

"Pretty please," Jillian pleaded while Riley clasped his hands together as if in prayer. Even as Jake smiled at their tactics, so similar to the ones he and Dean had employed in childhood, he held firm.

"Next trip," he promised. "Caro and I are going to see about her car."

"We won't be gone long," she assured

them. "Go finish your snowman. By the time you're putting on the carrot nose, we'll be back. Then it will be your turn."

Despite their objections and bitter complaints, they complied.

"Need help getting up on the seat?" Jake asked.

"You mean I don't get to sit in the back and burrow under a wool blanket?"

He shrugged. "Suit yourself."

"I was kidding, Jake. And, yes, I do need some help getting up on that bench."

He came around behind her. Resting his hands on her waist was torture, pure and simple, which perhaps explained why, as soon as he was seated next to her, he blurted out, "So, why no divorce?"

She turned to face him, clearly startled by the bald question.

"I...I..." Her eyes narrowed then. "What does it matter to you? No harm, no foul, remember? It was just a kiss."

He gritted his teeth and slapped the reins. As Bess began to plod through the thick snow, he thought sourly that there was nothing quite as unpleasant as having his words thrown back in his face.

But what he said was, "I'm curious is all. I was a cop, remember?"

"Is that the only reason?"

"For now," he allowed. "So?"

She stared straight ahead. "It's complicated."

"It's always complicated, Caro. I think, at the very least, you owe me some answers after last night."

Her cheeks turned pink. "Ask another question then."

"Okay, do you love him?"

"You don't pull any punches," she muttered after blowing out a breath that turned white in the frigid air.

"Well?"

"No. I did once…or at least I thought I did. But now…after everything that's happened, no."

That should have made Jake feel better, but it didn't. It brought him back to his first question, which she'd already ducked. So, he asked instead, "What does he do for a living?"

"He runs his family's investment firm. It's a Fortune 500 company. He's been at the helm since his father died right after Truman graduated from college."

"Let me guess. Harvard?"

"Yale, actually."

"Old money?"

"Very. The Wendells trace their wealth back a good five generations, from what I've been told. Think railroads."

No wonder Caro had said her mother-in-law didn't think she was good enough for her son. Even the average debutante would have trouble measuring up. He whistled between his teeth.

"How did you meet him?"

"At my job, interestingly enough. Every Wendell since the turn of the previous century has attended the academy where I worked. I already mentioned that his generous donation is responsible for the new science wing."

"And your loss of a counseling job that they promised to hold open for you."

"Yes." She cleared her throat. "Anyway, every spring they have an alumni dinner. The staff is invited and encouraged to attend. We mix and mingle, remind the guests of the school's virtues and extol any new programs to ensure they continue to donate their money and that succeeding generations of their families continue to enroll. Truman was there."

"And you mixed and mingled."

"There was a little more to it than that, but yes. He dropped by the school the following Monday and asked me out."

"Did you feel pressured to date him?" He wanted her to say yes. But she shook her head.

"No. In truth, I was flattered by his attention."

Jake glanced sideways in time to catch her frown.

"And maybe I wondered a little why someone like him was interested in someone like me."

"That's a no-brainer. Why wouldn't he be? You're beautiful, smart, sexy…." He let the adjectives trail away with his frozen breath and returned his attention to the snowy road.

It was a moment before Caro continued.

"Anyway, before I knew it, our courtship had begun in earnest. I wasn't sure I was ready for such a serious relationship, but he was so attentive and thoughtful. He said all the right things. He made grand, romantic gestures. My friends and coworkers adored him and his determination to take care of me. When he proposed, saying yes seemed like the right decision. I wanted so desperately to have a family again. I was so…alone."

Jake closed his eyes as understanding dawned. "This was right after your parents died, wasn't it?"

"Yes."

When she'd needed time, Truman had pressed his advantage. She'd said the man could be manipulative. No doubt he'd found a grieving young woman easy to convince of her good fortune. Jake also knew from his years of police work that some men liked to feel as if they were a savior of sorts. Hell, some of the guys he knew had joined the force for that reason. It was a fine line to walk between wanting to help people and wanting them to be beholden to you. He'd bet his severance that Truman fell into the latter category.

"Things were okay between the two of us at first, good even," Caro was saying. Her tone turned rueful when she added, "Especially when his mother wasn't around, which unfortunately wasn't often. But gradually he became more and more controlling.

I passed it off as caring at first. But as my grief began to fade I found it irritating.

"I started to wonder if I'd made a huge mistake, but then Cabot came along, and I was determined to try to make things work. Not only for my son, but for me. I didn't want to fail at marriage."

"I know the feeling," Jake said, thinking of how he'd tried to convince Miranda to go with him for counseling, and that was before he'd known she was pregnant. "What made you decide to leave him?"

"It wasn't one thing. It was a lot of little things that were made all the worse when his mother moved in with us."

He squinted at her sideways. "That couldn't have been fun."

"No. Susan pretty much took over. And when I complained, Truman took her side."

"So, is she moving out?"

Caro frowned. "My mother-in-law?"

"Yeah. Is that why you agreed to go back to your husband?"

Sleigh bells jingled in rhythm with Bess's muffled hoofbeats. Overhead, a crow's guttural cry rent the air. Still, Caro said nothing as she sat with her head bowed, studying her mittens.

"Is this another one of those questions you don't want to answer?" he said softly.

"I'm going back because of my son."

Her head lifted and he saw the tears. They tracked down her cheeks, dripped from her chin. He wasn't sure he understood their exact origin, but he knew he couldn't stand to see her so destroyed.

"Whoa!"

The big horse stopped. Caro continued to cry.

"It's...it's okay." But her tears dripped unabated. "Hey, you don't need to cry," he said a little more gruffly than he'd intended, in part because he felt both helpless and like an ogre for pressing her to answer questions that obviously caused her such pain.

As he had the night before, he wrapped his arms around her, and pulled her to him. She collapsed against his own battered heart.

"I know you don't want to fail at marriage, and...and I can say from a personal standpoint that I think kids deserve two parents under the same roof whenever practical or possible. But if you don't love him, if he makes you so damned miserable, Caro, your son is going to wind up miserable, too."

"I know that."

"Then why?"

"You don't understand. If I don't go back, I won't see my son. At least not every day. I'll lose him to Truman. And his mother. I won't let that humorless, judgmental old snob raise my child."

"Custody will be for a judge to decide."

Caro shook her head. "Every judge in town knows the Wendells. I'm pretty sure every judge in Vermont does. And they've benefited from the Wendells' generous campaign contributions over the years."

"The law is supposed to be impartial," Jake said, even though he knew that wasn't always the case. Deep pockets had a way of skewing verdicts and judgments.

Caro apparently knew it, too. "I haven't got the money to fight him, Jake."

"But I do."

His words seemed to echo over the frozen earth as she gaped at him.

"The department's payout was more than generous, especially since I've invested it wisely." He tilted his head to one side, considering. "Well, other than the inn. That's a gamble. Who knows if it will ever pay off?"

"It will. You'll make it shine again." But that wasn't why Caro straightened in her seat to study him. Good God. Jake meant it. He was absolutely serious when he said he would bankroll her legal fees. Of the dozens of thoughts and questions buzzing in her head, the one she gave voice to was: "Why would you do that?"

"I know how it feels to lose a child."

His answer surprised her almost as much as his offer. "I didn't think…I didn't realize you and Miranda had—"

"We didn't." A muscle worked in his jaw before he continued. "Miranda and I didn't get to fight over custody. She made sure of that with an out-of-state abortion just before our divorce was final."

"My God. Jake, I'm so—"

He cut her off again. "Me, too. I wake up every day sorry that my son or daughter never got a chance to draw breath." He reached for her hands then and squeezed them through the leather of his gloves and the knitted wool of her mittens. "If you want to fight for your son, Caro, I'll help you do it."

His offer was almost too good to be true, which was why she hesitated. "I don't know."

"Because of my reputation back in Buffalo?"

"Of course not." But then she reconsidered her hasty reply. "If Truman and his mother got wind of the incident, Jake, they would use it, no holds barred. You and your family could very well wind up in the media spotlight all over again."

It was just what he'd moved to Vermont to avoid. She expected him to back down. What he said was: "Who says he'll find out I'm the one funding your lawyer bills?"

"But…" For a moment, she'd thought Jake was offering more than his financial help. Attraction aside, why would he want to take on a ready-made family? Especially when it was clear he was still grieving his unborn child. She tried on a smile. "Thanks. I'll need to think about it."

"Okay. It's not a limited-time offer. Let me know when you decide." He slapped the reins against Bess's wide back. "Giddyap, girl." To Caro, he said, "Your car should be around the next curve."

The ride back to the inn was accomplished in silence, and no wonder, given all that already had been said.

Caro's mind was humming. She couldn't accept Jake's money, other than as a loan. It was an option she hadn't thought of before, knowing that no bank would consider her a good risk with a part-time job and little else to recommend her.

She'd seen nothing from her parents' estate. Most of it had gone to settle bills and other debts. The small amount she'd received from the sale of their house after taxes and the remaining balance they'd owed, she'd used for her wedding, considering it her dowry. At the time, she'd refused to go to Truman as a pauper, especially given his mother's opinion of her. Now she bitterly regretted her decision.

She and Jake had rescued both of her bags from her car, which was still all but buried in the snow. The road had yet to be plowed, as well. Which meant time was ticking. Truman had given her a reprieve before he went to file the legal paperwork, but for her own peace of mind, she had to be on her way to Burlington as soon as possible.

The inn came into view. It really was lovely, Caro thought, taking a moment to admire not only the bones of the building, but the scenery. Once Jake's renovations were complete, the place wouldn't hurt for business, whatever the season. Of that, she was certain.

She turned to tell him as much when a snowball caught him smack in the middle of his chest. It was then that she spied the children and their parents standing amid the towering maples and pines.

"Riley did it! Riley did it!" Jillian danced in place as much as her bulky, lavender snowsuit allowed.

"Son, how many times have I told you not to do that?" Dean began. His voice was surprisingly stern until he added, "If you're going to lob a snowball at someone you aim higher. Like this." He bent down, scooped up some snow and fired off a shot that took off Jake's hat.

"Tell me you didn't do that." Jake's tone was lethal.

"Oh, I did that, brother. I did that." Dean's grin was as wide and as childlike as his pre-school-aged son's was.

"Do it again, Daddy!" Riley encouraged, clapping his mitten-covered hands together in excitement.

"We're in for it now," Bonnie said, but she was smiling, too. And no wonder given the hard-packed sphere of white in her hand.

With an unholy shriek, she let it fly, knocking the knit cap clean off her husband's head.

"Whose side are you on?" he demanded comically as he plucked his hat from the snow and slapped it against his thigh.

"I'm on Caro's and Jilly's, of course. Come on, Caro. Hop down."

"Ah." He nodded. "Guys versus girls?"

"Only if you big, strapping hunks think you're up to it," she taunted.

"What's the prize this time?" Dean wanted to know. His expression turned lecherous.

Jake's gaze wasn't on his brother. He was watching her. Caro felt her face begin to heat and was relieved when Bonnie replied, "How about losers make the winners hot cocoa and serve it to them in front of the fire?"

"Fine by me," Jake said on a shrug. "Caro knows how I prefer mine."

She ignored the heat that shimmied up her spine and concentrated on his presumption that her team would lose. "Talk about being pompous."

"We'll see." She was too busy watching him wink to realize he'd scooped up the remains of the snowball that had struck him in the chest. Before she knew it he'd given her a "face wash" with it and was hopping down from the sleigh.

"This means war," she declared.

The next thing Caro knew, they had divided into a pair of teams and snowballs were flying all over the place. The women and Jillian were hunkered down behind a fallen tree. While Jillian packed ammunition, Caro and Bonnie went on the offensive.

"What in the heck was that?" Bonnie demanded between giggles as one of Caro's snowballs hit the ground nowhere near its intended target.

"I'm a bit rusty. It's been a while."

"Well, get un-rusty and fast. I'm not serving Dean hot cocoa today. That man's ego is big enough already." The insult, however, was delivered with affection.

"We're holding our own," Caro replied as a snowball disintegrated on the tree just behind her.

"Oh, yeah. You think so? Then I have just one question for you."

"What?"

"How does Jake take his cocoa?"

That spurred her into action. "Who is that hiding behind the rear of the sleigh?" she asked.

"I think it's Dean, although it's hard to tell since he left off his hat and they both have the same hair color. Feel free to blast away."

"Just don't hit Riley," Jillian said sincerely. "He can't help it that he's a boy."

"I'll do my best," Caro vowed.

"Your best hasn't done us much good so far," Bonnie groused.

"True, but I have a feeling this will." She whipped off her hat and waved it in the air like a flag of surrender as she stood. "Wait. Don't shoot. Please, don't shoot."

Jake appeared from his hiding spot. "What's wrong?"

"This." The snowball left her hand at lightning speed. Too bad her aim still stank. It struck the ground five feet to his left. But while he stood there gaping and incredulous, Jillian and Bonnie pelted him. With a two-fingered salute, he crumpled into the snow.

From his prone position, Jake told Dean and Riley, "It's up to you guys now."

They gave it their best, but then went down in defeat, mostly because Riley wanted to switch sides.

"You can't switch sides midwar," Caro heard Dean tell the little boy. "Besides, they're girls."

"They're winning, Daddy."

"I'm not raising a fool," Bonnie yelled. "Our son wants to be with the winners."

"Can we call a cease-fire?" Dean wanted to know.

"Only if it still comes with you guys serving us hot cocoa."

"Give it up, Dean. Even Riley knows we're done for." Jake stood and brushed the worst of the snow from his clothes.

Caro laughed, feeling younger and more carefree than she had in months...years. It wasn't all the result of the spontaneous snowball fight, she knew. It was Jake, these feelings he inspired and, of course, his offer.

Hope, that was indeed what this holiday was about.

While Bonnie herded a sullen Riley and jubilant Jillian back to the inn—with a rain check on the sleigh ride since they were too cold now to stay out much longer—Dean saw to Caro's bags. That left Caro to help Jake take Bess and the sleigh around back. Once the horse was relieved of her harness, rubbed down and settled into her stall with some feed, they started for the house.

"I can't believe you cheated," Jake muttered.

"I didn't cheat. I employed strategy."

"You tricked me."

"Yes. But you fell for it. Still, I'm sorry."

"Liar. You're not the least bit sorry."

"No." Laughter shook her shoulders. "You know what they say—all's fair in love and war."

They both sobered, and even though they'd reached the back entrance, they remained outside on the steps, Caro one stair higher and leaning against the rail.

Jake pulled the glove off his right hand and ran his bare knuckles over the slope of her cheek. "I like seeing you like this."

"How?" she whispered.

"Happy, laughing and not so damned desperate. You're beautiful, you know. Especially when you smile."

His chin angled up and he leaned toward her, slowly. Giving in to desire mere inches at a time. They shouldn't. Couldn't. Even so, Caro's chin angled down on a sigh. His mouth was a whisper away from hers when the back door opened. Riley stood there in his stocking feet, hair sticking up at odd angles from the hat he'd been wearing.

"Are you going to kiss her, Uncle Jake?" the little boy wanted to know.

"N-no," he sputtered. "I was…Caro has a lash in her eye. I was just seeing if I could get it out."

"Oh." Riley nodded, satisfied with the explanation. Caro expelled the breath she'd been holding until he added, "Daddy said you were going to kiss her."

Laughter rang out from behind him. Caro felt mortified. Jake looked ready to explode. Riley was grinning from ear to ear. And when they stepped inside, Dean wore the same expression.

His brother's delight was short-lived. Doreen came into the back entryway with her hands fisted on her hips and a look of displeasure turning down the corners of her mouth.

"What's this Bonnie tells me about hot cocoa?"

"We waged a snowball war," Jillian said as she lined up the boots on the mat by the door.

"I lost. Next time, I don't want to be on Daddy and Uncle Jake's team," Riley whined.

"Smart boy," Doreen replied, patting one of his rosy cheeks.

"Now we have to make hot chocolate

and serve it to them and everything," Riley wailed.

"No being a sore loser. Come on now." She clapped her hands together. "Let's get to it."

"You're not going to make the cocoa, are you?" Bonnie asked from behind Doreen.

"No." The older woman pursed her lips. "In fact, now that I think of it, I'm entitled to a little pampering myself. So, it was men against women?"

"That's right."

Turning, Doreen hollered, "Martin!"

"Uh-oh. Dad's not going to be very happy with us," Jake muttered.

"Speak for yourself," Dean groused. "I'm not the one who went all soft at the sight of a pretty lady."

"I'm not sure how to take that," Bonnie muttered.

"You know what I mean, hon."

"Uh-huh." She crossed her arms over her chest. "Be sure to put at least half a dozen mini-marshmallows in my cup."

"Oh, and have him add a splash of peppermint schnapps," Caro supplied helpfully. "Jake has a bottle in the kitchen cupboard."

"Ooh, I like that idea," Bonnie said, following a grumbling Dean down the hall. The kids tagged behind them, which left Jake and Caro alone amid the dripping boots and soggy outerwear.

She sat down on the bench that stretched along one wall and tried to remove her boots. Anything to keep her mind off Jake…and his mouth…and the kiss they shared the night before…and that almost kiss on the steps a moment earlier.

"Here. Let me help you with that," he offered when she couldn't quite manage the zipper down the front of the boots.

Jake knelt down in front of her and loosened the ice-encrusted zippers. He didn't stop there, though. He pulled the boots off her feet, set them aside and then gave the arches of her feet a slow once-over that had her toes threatening to curl. Even through two pairs of thick socks, Caro swore she could feel the warmth of his hands.

"Th-thanks," she stammered. "I believe the deal was hot cocoa, you know. Not a foot rub."

"Consider this a bonus." He tilted his head to the side. "Dean got it right, you know."

Her breathing hitched. "Oh?"

"I do have a soft spot where you're concerned."

"Jake." His name came out as a breathy whisper.

"I can't explain it, Caro." He shrugged and rose to his feet. "I'm a facts kind of guy. I think that's why I went into police work in the first place. I go where the evidence leads me. But in this case…" He shrugged again.

Caro rose, as well. "I'm not a case, Jake."

"I know that. *Believe me,* I know." He scrubbed a hand over the back of his neck in frustration. "I guess what I'm trying to say, and botching it badly, is that the way I'm acting, well, it's very out of character for me. Like outside on the steps just now. I wanted to kiss you. I would have, too, if Riley hadn't opened the door.

"And last night, in the kitchen, and today on the sleigh ride, I told you things I don't usually talk about. Things I don't share with anyone."

"I feel privileged."

"Privileged," he repeated, and shook his head.

"What I mean is—" she blew out a breath "—I feel it, too, Jake. Everything has happened so quickly between us. I feel like I did in my car while I was waiting for the skidding to stop. Where does *this* stop?" She motioned between the two of them.

"And if it doesn't stop, where does it go? Where can it go?" He seemed to be posing the question to himself as much as Caro.

"Jake! Get your worthless butt in the kitchen!" Dean hollered from the hallway. "The hot chocolate's not going to make itself, and Dad is claiming his role is purely supervisory since he got dragged into this mess."

"Be there in a minute."

"Now!" Dean howled with the authority of a drill sergeant.

"This conversation isn't over," Jake said to Caro as he left.

CHAPTER NINE

McCABE FAMILY TRADITION dictated that the men cleaned up after holiday meals since the women generally did all of the preparations. Today was no exception. Caro felt a little guilty since Doreen hadn't allowed her to help out in any fashion. So, when she noticed first Martin and then Dean duck out of the kitchen, she decided to check on Jake's progress.

He was at the sink, up to his elbows in soapsuds. A stack of dirty pots and pans was to his left while clean plates were drying in the rack to his right.

"It looks like you've been deserted," she said.

"Payback for the hot-chocolate incident," he grumbled with a shrug.

"Are you trying to make me feel guilty?"

"Depends." He squinted sideways at her. "Is it working?"

"Maybe a little." She picked up a dish towel from the counter and began drying the plates.

"You'd better not let my mother catch you doing that."

Caro smiled. "I won't."

They worked together in silence. She dried all of the plates and put them away, freeing up the rack for the serving dishes and finally for the pots and pans that he washed. The last piece of flatware had been returned to the drawer, and Jake was wiping down the counters when she decided to take a seat at the table. He joined her a moment later.

"Thanks."

"You're welcome. It was the least I could do, since I was sort of at fault."

A grunt served as his reply. Then, "You look nice, by the way."

"It feels good to be wearing something other than a robe or ruined wool."

After returning with her bags, she'd changed into fresh clothes—a flowered silk blouse and a slim skirt that she'd paired with peep-toe pumps. The outfit was a little fancy for the occasion, even if it was Easter

Sunday, but everything in her bag was on the fancy side.

Whereas the Wendells dressed for dinner even if it was being served in their own dining room, the McCabes didn't stand on formality. Jillian had insisted on wearing the frilly pink frock Bonnie had brought for Mass, making Caro feel less self-conscious. They hadn't been able to go, of course.

Had Truman and Susan made it to church? If so, Caro imagined that poor Cabot fidgeted from beginning to end. He rarely could sit through the hour-long service, anyway. Add in the thought of the treats and toys waiting for him back home, and he'd never be able to remain still.

"You're smiling," Jake remarked.

"I'm thinking about Cabot. If Truman and his mother somehow made it to church today, I'm sure he was all over the pew, especially if he managed to filch a few jelly beans from his basket ahead of time."

"That's kids. I swear Riley and Jillian can't go five minutes without jumping or skipping or hopping on one foot. They need to be doing something at all times."

Her expression dimmed a bit. "They'd never remember to bring a book or small toy to occupy him. My mother-in-law claims that Truman could sit through the service as still as a soldier by the time he was out of diapers."

"A couple doses of cold medicine and every kid can do that."

Caro chuckled.

"What's he like?"

"Cabot?"

Jake nodded. "Yeah."

"Well, he's funny and sweet, and the cutest child ever born, of course."

"The most intelligent, too," he added for her benefit.

"So, you've read the advertisement I took out in the national newspapers." Caro laughed. "But seriously, he is very bright. I think he might be reading before he begins kindergarten. And he has a great sense of humor for such a little person. I love to hear his laughter."

Recalling it now, her mood turned melancholy.

"It will all work out."

"I wish I could be so certain."

"You're not helpless, Caro. You yourself told me that within five minutes of our meeting," he reminded her. "And you were

stranded in a snowstorm at the time and clos-
ing in on frostbite."

"Thanks," she said sincerely.

"For what?"

"Reminding me of that." Even so, she closed
her eyes. "God, Jake, I'm so confused."

"Because of me?"

"Yes," she admitted. These unexpected
feelings she had for him certainly complicated matters. But what she said aloud was,
"I'd resigned myself to going back, to making do and not fighting Truman and his
mother for custody because I didn't have the
resources."

"Then I guess I've given you something to
think about."

In fact, Jake thought, he'd given them both
something to think about, especially since
altruism wasn't his main motive for offering
assistance.

Sure, he didn't want to see Caro forced
to return to the husband she'd left and obviously didn't love any longer. From what she'd
said, it was debatable that she'd loved him in
the first place. The man had preyed on her
vulnerability, taken advantage of her grief.
It wasn't right that she should have to return

to him and live under her mother-in-law's thumb if she wanted to be near her child.

What kind of life was that for her? What kind of life was that for her son?

But other factors came into play, too. The most damning one was that Jake couldn't stand the thought of her with another man, even if that man was legally her husband.

He was past the point of questioning his attraction to Caro or how quickly things between them had blossomed. His father once told him that he knew the moment he spotted Doreen at a college party that she was the girl for him. Forty years later, no one could doubt the authenticity of their feelings.

But his father had been at a point in his life where he'd wanted and been ready to settle down. Jake couldn't say the same. His life was in chaos, every bit as broken-down and ramshackle as the inn he was restoring. What did he have to offer Caro beyond the financial means to mount a first-rate custody battle?

What did he *want* to offer her?

She wasn't the only one who was confused.

Jake had spent more than a year immersed in anger and pain, reeling first from the police department's betrayal and then from Miranda's. For the first time in a very long time he didn't want to hide away in Vermont—and, yeah, Dean was right; that that was what Jake had been doing.

Now, he wasn't sure what he wanted to do. Go back to Buffalo and restore his good name? Maybe return to police work there or in a suburban community? Or stay in Vermont and finish the inn, maybe even stick around long enough to see it opened?

He'd be closer to Caro here. And as far away as ever if she chose to stay married to Truman.

"Even if I hire a top-of-the-line lawyer, I could lose custody of Cabot," she was saying.

"Yes. You could." He wouldn't lie to her. He reached for her hand on the table and rubbed the work-roughened pad of his thumb over her smooth skin. "You have to decide if the risk is worth it."

The same went for him.

The children were already asleep when the power came back on later that evening. Between playing in the fresh air and a big meal, they'd petered out even before their regular bedtime arrived.

Riley nodded off in front of the fireplace as he listened to their grandfather read them a story. Jillian grew heavy-eyed soon after and put up only token protest when her mother told her to kiss her grandparents, father and uncle good-night.

The little girl melted Caro's heart when she included her in the ritual.

After kissing her cheek, Jillian said, "I'm glad you got stuck in the snow by us, Caro."

"I am, too."

"You're a lot of fun for a grown-up, even if you aren't the best shot with a snowball."

"My technique needs work," Caro agreed in sham seriousness. "Maybe you can give me some pointers tomorrow."

"Okay." With her arms still wrapped around Caro's waist, Jillian added, "You know, if you married my uncle Jake, you'd be part of our family and we would see each other again."

Bonnie coughed. "Jilly."

"What, Mommy? Isn't that how Miranda became my aunt?"

"Yes, but—"

"See." The little girl grinned and then added innocently, "Miranda and Uncle Jake aren't married now, which means he can marry you. I already like you better than I liked Miranda. She said me and Riley gave her migraines."

Not knowing what else to say, Caro replied, "Some adults are prone to those."

"I heard Mommy tell Daddy once that she had a cure for Miranda's headaches. A swift kick in—"

Bonnie clapped a hand over her daughter's mouth to keep her from finishing. Dean, meanwhile, sat on the couch cackling like a loon. Jake said nothing, but for just a moment he'd looked as if he might join in his brother's laughter.

"And on that note we're out of here," Bonnie said. "Good night everyone. I may or may not be back down after the kids are tucked in."

She sent an apologetic smile in Jake's direction.

"I'll carry Riley up for you," he said. "You go on ahead with the flashlight."

It was his way of smoothing out an awkward situation. Bonnie smiled gratefully.

The lights flickered on a few minutes later as Jake returned from upstairs. The living room's occupants sent up a cheer.

"Now we can check the news for road

conditions and travel information," Doreen said pragmatically.

Their return flight to Buffalo was scheduled for the next evening.

"Forget about road conditions and travel information," Martin piped up. He'd already found the television remote and had turned on the set. "There's a hockey game on."

"Who's Buffalo playing?" Jake asked.

"Toronto," Dean supplied.

"Ooh, this should be good." He rubbed his hands together and hunkered down on the couch next to Dean. "Did you see that hit their linesman put on Buffalo's center the last time the teams met?"

Dean nodded. "They're going to be out for blood."

With her hands on her hips, Doreen sighed. "Twenty minutes, Martin. And no more."

Buffalo was up by three goals against Toronto before Doreen finally wrested the remote from her husband's hands and switched it to The Weather Channel to catch the local forecast, which included a segment on current travel conditions.

"It looks like the airport is reporting delays, but at least it's open for business. It sounds like we might get out of here tomorrow after all." Doreen smiled at Caro. "And the main roads should be passable."

Which meant she would be on her way soon, too, assuming her car was drivable. "That's wonderful news."

She missed Cabot desperately, and Truman had made it clear that she had only one week to arrive in Burlington. But Caro was no longer quite so eager to be on her way. She understood why when her gaze connected with Jake's. His expression was not quite so guarded that she couldn't see the interest there.

The next day dawned as sunny as the previous one had. Caro was up early, determined not to be the last one downstairs again. She needn't have worried. Bonnie and Dean were the late-risers on this morning, looking suspiciously smug and satisfied as they came downstairs long after their children had awoken and been handed off to Grandma and Grandpa.

Caro might have found the couple's sly smiles and stolen glances sweet and romantic if she weren't steeped in sexual frustration.

The phone lines were still down, but around noon Orville Gray, the owner of the garage Caro had contacted, arrived at the inn courtesy of a high-riding, four-wheel-drive vehicle that would have been right at home at a monster-truck rally.

The good news? Her car would be towed to his garage for repairs. The bad news? He wasn't sure he had all the parts in stock that he needed.

"I can order them. But it could be a few days before I can get them," he told her.

"A few days?" Caro's heart bucked. Technically, she had the time. Truman wasn't expecting her until the end of the week. But she was eager to see her son. They'd already been separated for too long. And there was the not-so-small matter that Jake's family would be on their way today. Tonight, it would be just the two of them in the big, empty inn. "Isn't there anything you can do to get me on the road sooner?"

Orville plucked at one of the ends of his handlebar mustache. "Sorry, young lady. That's an older-model car and an import at that. I don't keep those parts in stock."

"I can take you to Burlington, Caro."

"No. I can't ask you to do that. Your family is here."

"They're leaving this afternoon. We can

head out first thing in the morning. And, for the record, you didn't ask. I offered. I told you the first night you were here that if you couldn't get to where you needed to be by the time you needed to be there, I would take you myself."

She nodded, recalling his words. She'd been desperate then. She felt desperate now for an additional reason. They were losing their chaperones.

The McCabes had a late-afternoon flight out of Montpelier's airport, which was a good thing since the airport in Burlington was still closed. The storm had hit that community far harder, in part because of its proximity to Lake Champlain. Indeed, the roads in Burlington remained in bad shape and people there were being advised not to drive on them unless necessary, leaving her to wonder if she and Jake would be heading out first thing in the morning after all.

Caro bid his family farewell and then stood out of the way as the McCabes said their goodbyes to Jake. They didn't indulge in the sterile air kisses the Wendells did. No, they grabbed hold of one another in fierce embraces. Kisses were exchanged. Backs slapped or patted. Promises elicited from Jake that he would come back to Buffalo for a visit soon.

"You're always welcome here," he reminded his parents afterward as Doreen dabbed at her moist eyes.

Martin nodded. "We know that. And don't think Mom and I won't come. We're happy to."

"Good." Jake's eyes were bright, as well.

Martin rested one of his big hands on Jake's shoulder. "If you want to stay here, if you think you can be happy here, then your mother and I are behind you one hundred percent, son. But no matter what some people have made you believe, you'll always have a place in Buffalo."

"Yeah! You can live with us, Uncle Jake," Jilly offered excitedly.

Not to be outdone by his sister's spontaneous invitation, Riley piped up with, "I want bunk beds in my room. If you come to live with us, Uncle Jake, I'll get Daddy to buy them and you can have the top one."

The offer had all of the adults laughing. Dean was the first to speak.

"You'd have to pay rent of course."

"And cook and clean every other week," Bonnie inserted.

"Gee, you make it sound so tempting," Jake grumbled good-naturedly.

"First week is free of charge," Dean replied. He grew serious when he continued. "You know Bonnie and I would love to have you. For a week…for longer."

Jake swallowed and nodded. "I know. Thanks."

Caro felt a lump form in her own throat as she watched the brothers embrace.

Bonnie wrapped Jake in another hug. "We aren't going to wilt under a little gossip. And just let a reporter ambush me again outside Jilly's dance studio. He'll be singing soprano afterward."

"I don't doubt it."

Doreen embraced him for a second time, too. Because Caro was missing her own son, she understood the ache in his mother's heart. "Be happy—whether here, in Buffalo or in Timbuktu. That's all I want for you. I just want you whole again."

"I'm getting there, Mom. I'm getting there."

She pulled back and bracketed his face in her hands. Her expression brightened.

"Before this weekend, I wasn't so sure. But now, I think so, too."

With that they filed out. Caro stood outside with him. As the rented, four-wheel-drive SUV pressed through the snow, she discreetly wiped away a tear. They were good people, kind people, and she'd treasured her time with them.

It should have felt awkward, she thought, standing on the front porch with Jake and waving goodbye as the vehicle drove away. But it felt right somehow. Indeed, for the first time since her parents' death, she could honestly say she felt as if she truly belonged somewhere. If only Cabot was here, she thought wistfully. Then it would be perfect.

"You have an amazing family."

"Yes, I do. I've missed them."

"And they've missed you. That much is obvious," she remarked innocently.

So it came as a surprise when his shoulders stiffened and he said defensively, "I've done what I've done to protect them, Caro."

"I'm not criticizing." She backed up a step before stopping, holding firm. "I know you see it that way, but they don't, Jake." She rested a hand on his arm. "They just miss you. They're concerned and confused.

Have you told them half the things you've told me?"

"I...I... That's not fair. I told you, you're easy to talk to."

Just as she thought. "What's not fair is keeping them in the dark. They will support you no matter what. They said as much just now."

"What would you have me do, Caro?" He threw his hands up in exasperation.

"It's not my place—"

"Oh, no. No you don't. Don't back down now."

"Okay, I think you should share more of your feelings with your family members, especially your parents. And I think you should go back to Buffalo and, I don't know, hold a press conference or whatever, and try to either clear your name or at least publicly offer your version of events. Express your sorrow. You've done that with me. And explain that you went to the address you were given. Yes, a mistake was made, and lives were lost and changed forever as a result of it. It's admirable for you to take responsibility. I'm not asking you to try to pass the buck. I don't think that's what your family wants, either.

They simply don't want to see you crucified unjustly and run out of town."

"I wasn't run out of town. I left of my own accord."

"Did you? It sounded to me like you left Buffalo because you felt you had no other choice. That's not exactly the same as operating under your own free will. Believe me, I know."

His emotions simmering, Jake stalked a few paces away. What she said wasn't outrageous or even much different from what Dean and his father had told him on countless occasions. They felt he'd been shoved under the bus as a result of political expediency.

"Why does this matter to you, Caro?" he asked, deciding to lay out his cards. "You've got enough on your plate to deal with."

"That's true enough. But…"

"But what?" He moved closer, crowding her space.

She didn't retreat. She held her ground and earned a little more of his respect and admiration when she poked him in the chest and declared, "I care about you, Jake. All right? I…care."

With those words, issued in an earnest tone, she took the wind right out of his sails.

What remained of his anger evaporated just that quickly and his heart squeezed, although why, he wasn't completely sure. Hell, when one got right down to it, *care* was a pretty tepid word. Under other circumstances and coming from another woman, it might have barely rated an eye roll. But Caro's expression, which was both challenging and sincere, made the otherwise pedestrian comment seem far more meaningful.

He cupped her cheek, resisted the strong urge to pull her into his arms for a kiss. "You would have stuck," he said slowly, thinking that despite all of the ugliness that went on back in Buffalo, she would have stood by his side.

Caro blinked in confusion.

"Never mind." He reached for her hand and gave it a squeeze, before turning to go back inside. "I care about you, too."

A little while later, Jake pulled on his coat and headed out to the workshop, determined to put some physical distance between him and Caro. He didn't trust himself alone with her. Not given how he was feeling at the moment. Once there, he picked up a chisel and set to work carving a design in a piece of wood he'd already cut with the idea of creating a new mantel for the fireplace in his room. The very room in which Caro would be sleeping again tonight.

Thinking about her body wrapped in his sheets sent him into full fantasy mode. He wanted to be there with her, his hands exploring every inch of her skin. Not surprisingly, he used too much force with the chisel and hammer, and the design was ruined. He stared at both tools, before tossing them aside. His frustration, however, had little to do with his clumsiness.

He spent another hour in the workshop, though he accomplished next to nothing. And he was cold, too, since he'd never bothered to stoke up the propane heater. His emotions had been running too hot at the start.

He returned to the inn through the back door. Strange how much bigger and quieter the place seemed now that his family was gone and it was just him and Caro. Jake tried to ignore the sexual tension that snapped in the air when he found her in the kitchen. She looked so right there. She had a dish towel wrapped around her waist. Its ends were tucked into the back of a pair of navy blue trousers. They were dressy compared to his faded denim, but he didn't hold that against them given the way the gabardine hugged her backside. The need he wasn't entitled to feel bubbled to the surface. As much as he might want her, he couldn't have her. The fact remained that, legally at least, she belonged to someone else.

"Are you hungry?" she asked. "I heated up some of the leftovers from yesterday."

He was hungry all right. But honey-baked ham, green-bean casserole and mashed potatoes, even the herb-infused kind made by his mother, weren't what had him salivating as he watched Caro stand in front of the inn's ancient stove.

If it were merely about sex, he probably could have sat at the table and forked up the meal she'd so thoughtfully reheated. But what Jake wanted from her went beyond sex. It was precisely that realization that had him saying, "I'm not hungry."

"Oh?" She frowned.

"Sorry. Maybe a little later." He hitched a thumb over his shoulder. "I need to see about the…about the…plumbing in the hall bathroom."

A pair of finely arched brows lifted. She didn't believe him. And no wonder.

"I think Riley put something down it. The toilet is slow to flush."

"I see." She nodded, letting him off on the lie. "Well, how about if I put a plate together for you and cover it in tinfoil? That way it will be here waiting when you're ready."

"Thanks."

When he was ready...

A lot of things were waiting for Jake when he was ready. Decisions that needed to be made, changes he needed to accept and a past whose ghosts needed to be exorcised.

He went upstairs, bypassing the bathroom that he'd claimed required attention. When he reached his bedroom, he stepped inside and inhaled deeply once he caught the light scent of Caro's perfume. Earlier, he'd thought she'd put her stamp on the place and that was without some of her personal effects lying about. The photograph in the small silver frame on the bedside table caught his attention.

Cabot.

Jake picked up the picture as he settled on the edge of the mattress. The kid was adorable, no two ways about it. His chubby cheeks sported matching dimples. Jake saw a lot of Caro in the shape and color of the little boy's eyes. And that chin. It was a miniature version of hers. From his wide smile, Jake imagined he'd been laughing when the shot was taken. Earlier, Caro had remarked on Cabot's wonderful laugh.

Like mother like son, Jake thought, though hers was rusty from little use. Much as his had been. Until this weekend. Even his mother had noticed the change in him.

He set the photo aside and took out his journal, not intending to write in it, so much as to read from it. But in the end, he wound up with a pen in his hand and a jumble of words in his head waiting to spill free.

If you were here I would be apologizing to you. I haven't set a very good example. I felt justified in coming to Vermont. And, don't get me wrong, I don't regret it. I like the inn and the mountains and the slower pace of life. But your uncle was right about my reasons for leaving Buffalo. As much as I wanted to believe it was solely to protect everyone I loved from more gossip and scorn, I also did it because I couldn't face everything that had happened.

I still think about that woman and her daughter. I can still see the look of horror on their faces in that split second before they died. But they weren't the only innocents I failed to protect. I failed you, too.

I think I could have stuck it out if it were only a matter of my reputation. It wouldn't have been easy, and I certainly hated seeing what it did to our family, but I'd never been a quitter before. Then, I found out about you. I found out about you and I lost you all in one fell swoop. It was a one-two punch and, weighed down by guilt and grief, I went down for the count.

So, I didn't leave Buffalo, as much as I ran. I see that now. But the pain has followed me every step of the way, mostly because I've refused to let it go.

I've refused to let you go.

The idea of you, anyway. There never was a you, except in my heart. That's where you'll remain. Always. But I need to let you go otherwise. For my own peace. It won't mean forgetting that you once existed. Just as I'll never forget that woman and her daughter. It will mean accepting what can't be changed. And moving forward. Life can't be lived in

the past. Nor can it be based on if-only.
I've finally figured that out.
Goodbye, my little angel.

A tear dripped onto the page. Just as his
tears had smudged the words in the first
entry about his child, they did so now. It
seemed fitting. A beginning and an ending.
And he found peace.

"Jake?"

He swiped at his damp cheeks and glanced
over to where Caro stood in the open doorway. "Yeah?"

"Sorry to interrupt. I thought you'd want to
know, the phone is working again. I picked it
up on the off chance a few minutes ago and,
presto, a dial tone."

He nodded. "Terrific. You can call your
son."

"Yes." She didn't smile though. "Is…is everything all right?"

"I think so." He closed the journal and
held it to his heart for a moment before returning it to the drawer. "I just needed to
take care of some unfinished business."

CHAPTER TEN

JAKE WAS IN THE LIVING ROOM when Caro padded down the steps later that evening. Officially, she'd already bidden him goodnight. But she'd spent a couple of hours pacing her room. Sleep was the last thing on her mind, in part because she knew he had something on his mind.

Unfinished business.

The look on his face, the tears that streaked his cheeks. God, how it tore at her, recalling his pain.

He stood at the mantel with his back to her. He wore only a simple white T-shirt that stretched taut across the wide expanse of his shoulders. His hips were narrow in faded blue jeans. She had little doubt he would look incredibly handsome wearing a police officer's uniform or dressed in a tailored suit. But he did fine things for denim.

"Jake."

He turned. "I thought you'd gone to bed hours ago."

"I couldn't sleep. I…I was worried about you."

He shook his head. "No need."

She didn't buy it. "You're hurting. Tell me. You know you can."

He studied her for a moment before nodding. "I was making a clean break when you came across me earlier. That's never easy."

"No." But she was far from satisfied with his explanation, so she waited.

"I've kept a journal, a diary you might even call it." Gruff laughter followed. "The department shrink suggested it as a way to vent my feelings during the internal affairs investigation. I didn't bother much with it until I found about Miranda and…and what she'd done to our child."

Caro swallowed. "So, you've written your thoughts down."

"More or less." He shrugged. "I've wondered what he or she would have looked like, what his or her personality would have been like. I've…I've written to this child who never even existed outside of my heart."

Hearing him say it had her heart breaking.

But, unable to gauge his emotions, she asked slowly, "Do you think that's wrong?"

"No. Not wrong. But you…you can't move forward when you haven't dealt with the past. I think we're both living proof of that, Caro, though for different reasons."

If he expected her to disagree, he was mistaken. Caro nodded.

"The only path is forward," she said.

"Forward," he agreed.

They eyed one another in the living room's dim light. His gaze dipped lower and lingered, making Caro aware that this evening she was wearing her own robe. It wasn't quite as matronly as Bonnie's had been. Instead of thick terry cloth, it was made of lavender silk that was edged in lace at both the collar and cuffs. It was layered over a nightgown in the same hue. The supple fabric caressed her body when she shifted her weight from one foot to the other. Behind him a log in the fireplace splintered in two, shooting out sparks.

Half a dozen of them seemed to land on her skin and that was before he said, "God, you're beautiful."

He crossed to her and his hands found her waist. Their callused palms snagged the expensive silk as he slipped them around her and pulled her closer.

His mouth found hers. This kiss was more urgent than the one from the other night, and no wonder. It was forbidden. Even so, she reveled in the stolen moment. She ignored the tug she felt when he loosened the belt to her robe. She allowed it when he slipped it from her shoulders. She nearly cried out when his hands brushed the sides of her breasts through the nightgown, not only because of the sensations his touch aroused, but because of the utter futility of this unprecedented desire.

His fingers pulled the thin strap of the silk chemise off her shoulder, which granted him greater access. His mouth lingered on her throat only a moment before dipping to the swell of her right breast. She trembled and fought the urge to guide him lower.

"Jake." Her breathing was labored, her voice barely audible. "Jake, we need to stop."

"I know." He bit out the words as his hands returned to the relative safety of her waist. Then he rested his forehead against hers. "God, I wish you were single right now."

As did she. Even so, she asked, "And if I were?"

He stepped back, shook his head. "I made a decision today. A pretty monumental one for me. I'm not going to live my life based on if-onlys any longer.

"I want you, Caro. I think… I think I may be falling in love with you," he staggered her by saying. "Which is why I'm going to ask you to go back upstairs now and not come down until the morning. Or else I have a feeling something will happen between us that we'll both regret. Because the fact remains you're not single."

How was it possible to be wounded and touched by the same words, Caro wondered?

She cupped his whisker-roughened cheeks in her palms. He was handsome all right. But his true beauty lay within. "I think I'm falling in love with you, too. You're a good man, Jake McCabe. I've told you that before. You are *exactly* the kind of man I want my son to grow up to become."

He pressed her hands tighter against his face for just a moment before pulling them away.

In a hoarse whisper, he said, "Go to bed now. Please. Or you'll be taking back that compliment."

* * *

The ride to Burlington seemed to take forever, Caro thought, which was both blessing and curse. She was loath to leave Jake, but the fact remained, she was returning to her husband.

God, she was confused. Not only about whether or not to accept Jake's financial offer, but about the man himself. They'd expressed their feelings for one another, and he'd said he was eager to accept his past and move on, but what did that mean?

All she knew for certain was that both of them were at crossroads in their lives. Whether or not they would wind up following the same path remained unclear.

The snow had been plowed down to the pavement at the estate on Lake Champlain. It was a beautiful place in a lush setting. It had never felt like home. In the summer, the landscaping was unparalleled on the lake. Ornamental shrubbery, rioting blooms and an immaculately groomed lawn that stretched down to a sandy beach on the lake at the home's back. Right now, everything was buried beneath snow...every bit as frozen as Caro's heart.

Susan opened the door as Jake carried her bags up the front steps.

"Caroline. How good to see that you've made it after your...ordeal. Truman told me all about your accident. How unfortunate."

"She almost died," Jake inserted.

Susan's sharp gaze turned to him, though she continued to address Caro. "And who might your escort be?"

"McCabe. Jake McCabe," he offered before Caro could. Truman materialized then, and Jake stuck out a hand. The two men shook as Susan looked on.

Caro was left to wade into the breach.

"Jake was kind enough to give me a ride to Burlington today when it became clear that my car wouldn't be ready. It's still in the shop," she said.

"Only because you insisted on leaving your Mercedes here," Susan said with a sniff.

Caro ignored her. Glancing around, she asked, "Where's Cabot?"

"Down for a nap," Susan replied.

Truman's gaze still on Jake, he asked, "And you know Mr. McCabe how?"

"She's been staying with me for the past few days."

She wasn't sure whether to cry or throttle Jake for his reply.

"At his inn," she corrected. "His family was kind enough to include me in their Easter celebrations."

"Family? So, you're married." Truman's demeanor relaxed a little at the news.

"Actually, I'm divorced." Was it her imagination, or did Jake take delight in informing him of that? "My parents, brother, his wife and their kids were in town."

Truman and Susan both frowned. Clearly, they were not satisfied despite the volume of chaperones.

"Do you normally drive your guests long distances to their destinations, Mr. McCabe?" Susan asked.

"I couldn't say. Caro is actually my inn's first guest."

"Jake…er…Mr. McCabe isn't open for business. He only recently bought the place. It's under renovation," she clarified. "Even so, he was kind enough to let me stay."

"Indeed," Truman said.

"I really want to see Cabot," she said, trying not to sound as desperate as she felt.

"I told you, he's sleeping." This from Susan. "He was up much too early this morning. For the past few mornings, in fact."

"You should wake him. I bet he would love to see his mother," Jake said.

Her mother-in-law laughed then. "You have quite the champion here, Caroline."

Another time, she might have appreciated it when Jake said, "She prefers to be called Caro."

"Exactly what do you know of my wife's preferences, Mr. McCabe?" Truman asked.

Jake's gaze cut to Caro. "Not nearly enough."

A high-pitched squeal rent the air then. At the top of the elegantly curved staircase stood Cabot. His grin took up his entire face.

"Mommy! Mommy!"

"Cabot!"

They met at the midway point on the stairs, where Caro scooped him into her arms, hugging his chubby little body close to hers.

"I've missed you, baby. God, how I've missed you." She rained kisses on his cherubic face as she carried him downstairs.

"Who's this?" he asked, pointing to Jake.

"This is Mr. McCabe," Truman supplied.

"He was just leaving," Susan added.

Caro ignored them both. "Can you say hello to Mr. McCabe, Cabot?"

"Hello." After offering the greeting, her son dropped his head into the curve of her neck, suddenly shy.

"Hi, Cabot," Jake said. His tone was as warm and melodic as it was when he talked with his nephew and niece. "Your mom's told me a lot about you."

"Mr. McCabe helped me when my car got stuck in the snow."

"I missed you, Mommy," Cabot said again. "Don't ever leave me again."

"Never," she promised, her grip tightening. Over her son's shoulder, she saw Jake tense. But that didn't prevent Caro from saying "Never" a second time.

Jake nodded and reached behind him for the door handle. "I've got to be going. If you need anything..." He seemed to realize he'd gone too far. "If you think you left anything behind, let me know. I'll be happy to ship it to you."

And with that he was gone.

CHAPTER ELEVEN

TWO MONTHS WENT BY. The inn began to take shape. It helped that Jake worked on it day and night with a passion born of frustration and, it galled him to admit, heartache.

He missed Caro, in ways both large and small. He missed her laughter, her insight and her quiet compassion. He missed her companionship. And, he missed her physically. Though he'd washed the bedding from his room half a dozen times, he swore the scent of her still lingered on his sheets, making sleep all but impossible.

For the short span she'd been under the inn's roof, it had reminded him of the place it had been in his youth. At the time, he'd tried to attribute that to his family's presence. That wasn't the sole reason, he knew now.

Caro had forced him out of his self-imposed isolation. It had taken a stranger, and a desperate one at that, to make Jake reexamine his current life. No amount of bullying from Dean, no amount of pleading from his parents, had accomplished the same thing. But a few days with Caro, and he'd been forced to recognize his life's limitations and open his eyes to its possibilities.

Though it was killing him that she had yet to contact him, whether to let him know if she wanted his financial help or anything else, he would always be grateful he'd stumbled across her in that snowstorm.

He was making a place for himself here. Not just restoring the inn, but creating a home. He wasn't sure exactly when he'd reached the conclusion that he wanted to open the inn and stay to run it, only that life here amid the towering maples and mountains suited him.

Though he tried not to dwell on it often, he could picture Caro and Cabot here. Living together. A family of three...growing in number through the years. For now, though, that was a mere fantasy.

The phone rang just as he slumped down on his mattress, exhausted from another day's work. It was Bonnie.

"I was just thinking of you and decided to give you a call," his sister-in-law began.

"Is everything all right at home?"

"Oh, fine. Great, in fact. Jilly lost another tooth last week, and Riley went through kindergarten screening on Monday. The school says he's more than ready to start in the fall. When they asked him to count to ten, my little show-off did it in Spanish," she finished proudly.

"He's a bright kid. Gets it from you."

"Bless your brother, but don't I know it." Her laughter boomed through the line. When it subsided, she said quietly, "We got a card from Caro today. She and Jilly have been corresponding for a while now."

"Yeah?" He wasn't quite able to hide his interest.

Bonnie heard it. "She asked about you in her letter. Wanted to know if you'd been back to Buffalo."

"I've been busy with the inn. You should see it now. Fresh paint in every room, a new carpet runner on the stairs and the hardwoods have been refinished throughout."

"What about that banister?"

"Good as new. *I* could slide down it now."

"Is that all you've done?" she teased.

"No. I handcrafted new mantels for all of the fireplaces and finished up the last of the chairs for the front porch. There are eight in all."

She whistled through her teeth. "Well, I guess you really have been busy." Then, in a more serious tone, she asked, "Do you like it there, Jake?"

"I do."

"So, you plan to open the inn and…and welcome guests and everything?" Bonnie asked.

"I think so," he replied slowly.

"All by yourself?"

"I'll have to hire some staff."

"That's not what I meant."

"She's married, Bonnie. It's not as easy as calling her up and asking her out on a date."

"But you would if you could."

He remained silent. The fact was, if he could, he would do much more than that.

"She loves you, you know."

"She wrote that in a letter?" he asked.

"No. I figured it out on my own by watching the two of you at the inn."

"She's married," he said a second time, reminding himself as much as he was reminding Bonnie. "She needs to be the one to decide whether or not she wants to remain such. And she has a lot at stake."

"Custody of her son."

"Yes. It's her decision. She knows I'll support her whatever she decides."

"That's it? You're not going to do anything else?" Bonnie persisted.

"I'm doing it."

"Toiling at your inn, while Caro languishes in Burlington?"

It dawned on him then. "I need to have something to offer her," he said softly. "Not just the inn, but a clean slate."

"There are a lot of folks here in Buffalo who are still willing to champion your cause. So, when are you coming?"

It was time, he thought. And he was ready. Ready to go back to Buffalo, to face the public, the police department and the ghosts that haunted him.

"Expect me Wednesday evening."

Jake's meeting with city officials and his former superiors at the Buffalo Police Department on Thursday morning went better than he expected, and that was saying a lot.

Prior to the official sit-down, he'd met up

with the members of his old squad. They'd welcomed his return with whoops and hollers and multiple offers to buy the first round of drinks at a favorite watering hole after hours. Their enthusiastic welcome buoyed Jake's spirits.

"When will you be back in uniform?" one called as he started toward the door.

It was without regret that he said, "It's not going to happen, guys, but look me up if you ever get out to Vermont."

The mayor, the head of Internal Affairs and the chief of police were seated around a table in the conference room when Jake entered. The only person he didn't recognize was introduced as the city attorney. Unless he missed his guess, they thought he was considering some sort of legal action against the city.

"It's good to see you again, McCabe." This from Chief Edwin Dash, who divided a nervous glance between Jake and Mayor Charles Kersher.

The mayor, who was behind in the most recent poll of likely voters, didn't look the least bit happy to see Jake.

"Hello, Captain McCabe."

"Mr. Mayor."

Dash cleared his throat. "And you remember Bob Feldman from IA."

"I do."

Bob smiled as they exchanged a handshake. He could be hard-nosed and annoyingly anecdotal at times, but he was fair and apolitical, as his initial report, which had cleared Jake of wrongdoing, proved.

"Jake. There are a lot of people in this town who were hoping we'd seen the last of you. I was never one of them."

"Thanks, Bob."

The mayor frowned, as did the city attorney, Fred Hans, a portly gentleman with a bad hair comb-over.

The attorney was the first to speak after they took their seats around the table.

"As you know, the city offered you a lucrative sum to resign your position within the department. That amount was and remains nonnegotiable."

Jake ground his molars together before replying. "I'm not seeking a bigger payoff from the city, Mr. Hans." His gaze cut to the mayor's and the chief's before it settled on Bob's. "I'd like the Internal Affairs investigation reopened or another one launched. I want to know exactly how I was given the wrong address."

"Jake, we've been through this."

Jake talked over him. "I didn't misread it and it wasn't a simple case of transposed numbers or the right house number but the wrong street. It was out-and-out wrong. A woman and her child died as a result. The young cop who fired the fatal rounds killed himself. And I…I've decided I'm no longer willing to accept what I was told. I want to know what *really* happened."

"The city supported you both during and after the internal affairs investigation," the lawyer said. "You were on paid administrative leave and a press conference was called to announce the findings."

"I remember that press conference. As the saying goes, I was damned with faint praise." He turned to Bob then. "I'm not questioning your initial investigation, but I wonder if something might have gotten missed since the focus was on me."

"Who else should it have been on?" the mayor snapped.

Jake nodded. "It happened on my watch. For that, I'll accept responsibility. But if it was an error, human or computer, the department needs to figure out a way to ensure it doesn't happen again."

"Perhaps we can look into things again. I never felt I got full cooperation from everyone involved, but there was such a push to complete the investigation." Bob left it at that and glanced at the mayor. The mayor frowned.

"I don't want one word of this breathed to the media until you have something concrete," he warned the chief.

In other words, don't do anything to jeopardize further his chances for reelection.

That wasn't good enough for Jake. The chief and Bob were obligated to adhere to the mayor's wishes. Jake, who was no longer an employee of the city, felt no such compunction.

When he called a press conference for the following morning, Jake made it clear that his silence was over, his grief for the family was immense and that he wanted more answers than had been provided so far to ensure such a thing never happened again.

This time, he welcomed the media spotlight's glare.

"Don't touch that, Cabot!" Susan shouted as the little boy picked up a piece of driftwood that had washed up on the sandy shore in front of the Wendell home on Lake Champlain.

"It won't hurt him," Caro called to her mother-in-law, who was seated on the patio with Truman, enjoying lunch al fresco on this unseasonably warm September afternoon. "It's just a piece of driftwood." To her son, she said, "Let's pretend it's a pirate ship."

"Caro, don't encourage him. Who knows what he'll pluck off the beach next."

"Like a seashell or two," she muttered under her breath as Susan continued.

"No doubt it reeks of that unpleasant fish smell. You should take him inside at once and have him wash his hands."

Truman folded his newspaper and set it aside, finally deciding to weigh in. "Mother is right. It never hurts to err on the side of caution where germs are concerned."

It didn't surprise her in the least that he took her side. Nor did it surprise Susan, who smiled smugly. In the months Caro had been back, nothing had changed. Truman still treated her as a lump of clay to be molded, and his mother was ruling the roost.

"Be sure to have him use the antibacterial soap," Susan instructed.

Caro took Cabot inside, but not with the intention of scouring his hands. What's more, she'd smuggled in the driftwood, which she let him play with while she placed her call. She'd put off making the call since her return to her husband, though in truth she'd wanted to chase Jake down the driveway that day back in March and beg him to take her and Cabot with him.

Instead, she'd swallowed her pride and her tongue. For Cabot's sake, she'd tried not to rock the boat. But the boat was filling with water and her ability to bail was at an end. One way or another, this ship was going under.

After working up her courage to dial the number Jake had given her, it came as a huge letdown when she got a recording:

"You have reached the Second Chance Inn in Blakefield, Vermont. Unfortunately, we're still closed for renovations, but we will be open the second week in October, just in time for the fall colors. Visit our website for sightseeing information and room rates and to book a reservation online."

Disappointed though she was not to talk to him personally, it was hard not to smile.

Jake was taking a chance and opening the inn. Her heart swelled.

Caro glanced over to where her son sat on the floor, pushing the driftwood "pirate ship" over the waves of the Aubusson rug Susan had insisted on to replace the one Caro had picked out for the great room. God, what she would give for a crystal ball to know what the future held. But there was no way to know. She only knew she had to try.

CHAPTER TWELVE

JAKE WAS SWEEPING LEAVES off the front porch when he heard a vehicle coming up the drive. Probably a delivery. He'd been inundated with those the past couple of weeks as the grand reopening of the inn neared.

He glanced over his shoulder but instead of a delivery truck it was an older-model car. The driver looked somewhat familiar. No. It couldn't be, he thought as he leaned on the broom handle and waited for it to stop. But it was indeed Caro who was behind the wheel.

He grinned broadly, eager to take her into his arms, until he spied the little boy dozing in a car seat in the back. She had a life and a husband back in Burlington, and if her silence these past several months was any indication, she was keeping both.

He wanted to be happy for her, and happy

for her little boy, too. But his heart was still just a little too bruised where she was concerned. He still wanted her…both of them… for himself.

"Hello, Jake," she said as she stepped out. The breeze caught her long hair and pulled tendrils of it across her face. He pushed it aside, glad for the excuse to touch her, even if only briefly.

"This is a surprise."

"I probably should have called," she admitted.

"No. No problem." He glanced inside the car at Cabot. "He's tuckered out."

"Nap time," she explained.

"How's he doing?"

"Terrific. He's growing like a weed. At his last pediatrician visit he topped out on the chart for height." She motioned to the inn, then, and changed the subject. "I thought you were open for business."

"Not quite yet. Another couple days."

"I like the name, by the way. Second Chance Inn."

"It seemed to fit."

She nodded. "I heard that you'd gone back to Buffalo and tried to clear your name."

"That made the news in Vermont?" he asked in surprise.

"Not exactly. But I found some articles on the internet. I read they reopened the investigation."

So, she'd kept up on him. He thought that was a good sign.

"Nothing conclusive, yet, although the human error is no longer pointing in my direction."

"I'm glad."

"Better than that, I finally got a chance to talk face-to-face with the victims' family. Against the city attorney's advice, I met with the father."

Her expression sharpened. "And?"

"The man...he said he forgave the rookie and everyone else involved in the raid, including me, a long time ago. He said hanging on to those kinds of feelings doesn't do anyone a bit of good.

"Seeing how he could be so forgiving made it easier to forgive myself." He cleared his throat, but his voice still wavered a bit when he admitted, "And it helped me forgive Miranda for what she did to our child."

"Oh, Jake. I'm glad." She reached out and

squeezed his forearm. "You look…relaxed, happy."

"Pretty much," he agreed, although there remained one major blight on his peace—and she was standing before him.

The breeze sent the leaves he'd just cleared off the porch skittering back over the wooden boards. Futile, he thought. That's what this was. It was killing him, standing here talking to her, when what he really wanted was to pull her in his arms, kiss her, hold her, beg her to stay with him.

She motioned behind him to the inn. "The place looks incredible, by the way. Inside and out. I took the virtual tour offered on your website."

"That was Bonnie's idea."

"It's a good one."

He nodded and worked up a smile. "I took your suggestion, too." At her frown, he explained. "I hired someone to staff the front desk."

Caro's laughter drifted away on the breeze. "I noticed you're booked solid through the New Year."

"Don't be fooled. Half the rooms are rented by my family." He pushed at some leaves with the broom, mostly just to give his hands something to do. "So, where are you headed?"

"I'm on my way to Montpelier."

That surprised him. "Yeah?"

"A job," she said, and her smile bloomed. "I got my old job back in the public school. It's still only part-time, but…"

"Caro—"

She cut him off. "I left Truman. This time for good, Jake." Her gaze strayed to the car's window. "I'm going to seek full custody of Cabot."

"And you need a loan."

"Yes." Her smile trembled. "To start. I was hoping for a little more than that from you later on."

"Whatever you need from me, Caro, you've got it."

"Well, there is one thing." She licked her lips, exposing nerves. "You once mentioned you thought you were falling in love with me. Did you get over it?"

"Not by a long shot."

He let go of the broom handle so he could pull her into his arms. It clattered against the porch railing, causing Cabot to stir in his car seat. A pair of sleepy eyes opened, blinked.

"Where are we, Mama?" Cabot asked.

"I can answer that one," Jake said. "You're right where you belong."

EPILOGUE

IT TOOK A WHILE BEFORE Jake's statement proved true.

A year longer, in fact, during which Caro and her son lived in a small efficiency apartment in Montpelier. She didn't mind the wait. It gave her time to get to know Jake, the time that their initial whirlwind romance had lacked. Now, more than ever, she was sure of her feelings.

It also gave Jake and Cabot time to form a bond. They were a delight to watch together. Jake was so patient with the boy, so fond of showing him new things. So eager to pass on what his own father had passed on to him. Already, Cabot had a tool belt and could name all of the different kinds of saws Jake used in woodworking. He wasn't allowed to touch them, of course. And he was only allowed inside the workshop when Jake was with him, and then only to sit in a designated chair well out of harm's way.

Reservations at the inn remained strong. It was a rare weekend that found the Second Chance with a vacancy, and peak times, such as now with Vermont's colors in full glory, it was booked solid with a waiting list of guests hoping for a cancellation.

Jake's family came often from Buffalo. They doted over Cabot, who was made an honorary McCade long before Caro's divorce settlement and custody arrangement became final.

With the money Jake loaned her, Caro was able to hire an excellent lawyer.

"You've changed, Caroline," Truman had told her one day after depositions were taken.

"A little," she'd agreed. "But mostly you're finally seeing me as I really am and not as the woman you want me to be."

He'd frowned. But that appeared to be a turning point. Not long afterward, he'd backed down from his initial threat to see that their son was taken away from her completely.

Susan, of course, wanted to continue to

fight. For once, Truman appeared willing to go against his mother's wishes.

Maybe there was hope for him after all, Caro thought. Just not as her husband.

Through it all, Jake remained steadfast and as patient as a monk, even as the days passed, and their desire grew and frustration built.

Leaves skittered across the drive now as Caro pulled up at the inn. Jake and Cabot were outside. Cabot was playing in a freshly raked pile of leaves while Jake grinned. It was hard to believe she'd ever thought him brooding and cold. He smiled so much these days.

He sobered a bit when he spied her. He'd been waiting for her to return from the courthouse. She could have called with the news, but she'd decided to deliver it in person. It was too important.

"Mommy!" Cabot hugged her legs once she got out. They played in the leaves for a moment before she sent him inside to ask the inn's cook for some apple cider.

"How'd it go?" Jake asked once they were alone.

She blew out a breath, still reeling from the events of the day. "Divorce granted and I have full custody, although Truman will have visitation. Every other weekend and certain holidays."

"Are you okay with that?"

"More than okay. I won't deny Truman his right to see our son, and it would be wrong to deny Cabot a chance to spend time with his father."

"I love him, too, every bit as much as if he were my own. I always will."

"I know." She tipped her head to one side. "I have a question for you, Jake McCabe."

"A question?"

"How soon can we be married?"

His face split into a grin as he reached for her. "Is that a proposal?"

"If it is, you haven't answered the question. How soon can I become Mrs. Jake McCabe?"

"Not soon enough," he told her, lowering his head. "Not soon enough."

RIVA™

Cupcakes and Killer Heels
by Heidi Rice

Ruby Delisantro's usually in the driving seat when it comes to relationships, but after meeting Callum Westmore's bedroom eyes she's in danger of losing control and—worse—of *liking* it!

Sex, Gossip and Rock & Roll
by Nicola Marsh

Charli Chambers has *never* met someone as infuriating—or delectable!—as businessman Luca Petrelli. Can she ever get close enough to the real Luca for their fling to be more than just a one-hit wonder?

The Love Lottery
by Shirley Jump

When her name is unexpectedly drawn in the town's love lottery, uptight Sophie Watson's horrified to be matched with smug-but-sexy Harlan Jones! A week of dating him will be *terrible*—won't it?

Her Moment in the Spotlight
by Nina Harrington

Mimi Ryan's debut fashion show is her dream come true. If she's being bossy then grumpy photographer Hal Langdon will just have to live with it! It's a shame she can't get his strong arms or teasing smile out of her mind…

On sale from 6th May 2011
Don't miss out!

Available at WHSmith, Tesco, ASDA, Eason and all good bookshops

www.millsandboon.co.uk

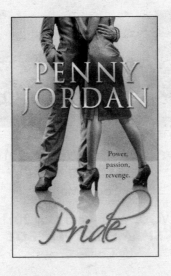

BAD BLOOD

A POWERFUL DYNASTY, WHERE SECRETS AND SCANDAL NEVER SLEEP!

VOLUME 1 – 15th April 2011
TORTURED RAKE
by Sarah Morgan

VOLUME 2 – 6th May 2011
SHAMELESS PLAYBOY
by Caitlin Crews

VOLUME 3 – 20th May 2011
RESTLESS BILLIONAIRE
by Abby Green

VOLUME 4 – 3rd June 2011
FEARLESS MAVERICK
by Robyn Grady

8 VOLUMES IN ALL TO COLLECT!

2 FREE BOOKS
AND A SURPRISE GIFT

We would like to take this opportunity to thank you for reading this Mills & Boon® book by offering you the chance to take TWO more specially selected books from the Riva™ series absolutely FREE! We're also making this offer to introduce you to the benefits of the Mills & Boon® Book Club™—

- **FREE home delivery**
- **FREE gifts and competitions**
- **FREE monthly Newsletter**
- **Exclusive Mills & Boon Book Club offers**
- **Books available before they're in the shops**

Accepting these FREE books and gift places you under no obligation to buy, you may cancel at any time, even after receiving your free books. Simply complete your details below and return the entire page to the address below. You don't even need a stamp!

YES Please send me 2 free Riva books and a surprise gift. I understand that unless you hear from me, I will receive 4 superb new books every month for just £3.99 each, postage and packing free. I am under no obligation to purchase any books and may cancel my subscription at any time. The free books and gift will be mine to keep in any case.

Ms/Mrs/Miss/Mr _____ Initials _____

Surname _____

Address _____

_____

_____ Postcode _____

E-mail _____

Send this whole page to: Mills & Boon Book Club, Free Book Offer, FREEPOST NAT 10298, Richmond, TW9 1BR